D0407385

Little Peach

PEGGY KERN

BALZER + BRAY

An Imprint of HarperCollins *Publishers*

Balzer + Bray is an imprint of HarperCollins Publishers.

Little Peach
Copyright © 2015 by Peggy Kern
All rights reserved. Printed in the United States of America.
No part of this book may be used or reproduced in any manner
whatsoever without written permission except in the case of brief
quotations embodied in critical articles and reviews. For information address HarperCollins Children's Books, a division of
HarperCollins Publishers, 195 Broadway, New York, NY 10007.
www.epicreads.com

Library of Congress Cataloging-in-Publication Data
Kern, Peggy.
  Little Peach / Peg Kern. — First edition.
    pages cm
  Summary: Hospitalized in Brooklyn, New York, fourteen-year-
old Michelle recalls being raised in Philadelphia by a loving
grandfather and drug-addicted mother before running away
and getting lured into prostitution.
  ISBN 978-0-06-226695-8
  [1. Prostitution—Fiction. 2. Drug abuse—Fiction.
3. Runaways—Fiction. 4. African Americans—Fiction. 5. Family
problems—Fiction. 6. New York (N.Y.)—Fiction.] I. Title.
PZ7.K457835Lit 2015   2014022114
[Fic]—dc23   CIP
                                                               AC

Typography by Torborg Davern
15 16 17 18 19   CG/RRDH   10 9 8 7 6 5 4 3 2 1

First Edition

For the missing

This is reality, whether you like it or not. All those frivolities of summer, the light and shadow, the living mask of green that trembled over everything, they were lies, and this is what was underneath.

This is the truth.

—WILLA CATHER, *MY ÁNTONIA*

Little Peach

1

CONEY ISLAND HOSPITAL

Coney Island, New York

You ask me to tell you the truth, but I'm not sure you'll believe me, even though I've practically killed myself to find you.

"It's okay," you promise, and a small laugh slips out of me despite my broken teeth. You watch me, then smile softly and sit down at the edge of the hospital bed.

My eyes are so swollen, I can only see pieces of you at a time: your grayish-brown hair pulled back into a sloppy ponytail, your dark round eyes, your white coat with a plastic card clipped to the pocket. I can't read your name, but I know it's you. I remember your face. You gave me your card two days ago when I came into the emergency room with Kat.

Daniela Cespedes, CSW. You're the one I came to find. You're the one I've bet my life on.

My eyes are huge and my front teeth are cracked and there's a gash on the right side of my leg. You probably don't recognize me. Maybe you don't remember me at all: the girl in the red shorts who ran in here two days ago, screaming like crazy with my crazy bleeding friend.

But you talked to me that day. You saw my tattoo and said, *Maybe I can help*, and Kat started crying and told you to shut the hell up.

Kat's gone now. And here I am, bleeding just like her. I got nothing left but your card and the clothes they cut off me in the ambulance.

A nurse walks in and pushes a needle into the tube that sticks out of the back of my hand. I can't stop shaking. Bone shaking. She adjusts the bed and I groan as it moves. Then she covers me with another thin blanket.

"Five minutes, okay?" she says to you. "We need to get that leg cleaned up."

The doctor said my leg's pretty bad. They can't fix it unless they operate. I'll be here for a few days—inside, and safe—with enough time to tell you what happened.

"What's your name?" you ask.

It's not an easy question.

I won't tell you everything. Some things I won't talk about. But I gotta start somewhere, so I take a deep breath and open my mouth.

"Michelle," I whisper. The name squeezes off my swollen tongue.

"Hi, Michelle," you say gently. "I'm Daniela."

I know.

"I'm with the crisis team here. It's my job to help you, okay? So I'm going to ask you a few questions. How old are you, sweetie?"

I can tell from your face that you're worried. I must look pretty bad.

"Fourteen."

Your eyes go soft and you let out a deep sigh. The way you look at me makes me feel like a little kid. I pull up the blanket to my chin. Suddenly, I just want to sleep.

I'd give anything to freeze this moment—before you know the truth. Right now you think I'm a nice girl who got jumped or robbed or worse. I must seem like a good kid. Like I got a worried mom somewhere.

Then you start to ask questions I can't answer.

"What's your address?"

"Your phone number?"

"Who do you live with?"

I shake my head no each time and try to keep my eyes open. I feel myself sinking. A deep warm sea of clean and quiet so familiar that I almost say *hello*.

Tonight, after it was over and the ambulance came, I kept thinking about Grandpa. All these people fussing over me, rushing around, telling me it would be all right even though it probably won't. Grandpa would have liked that.

I thought about Mom too. For a second I pictured her here, at the hospital waiting for me, which is crazy, of course, 'cause she's got no idea where I am and couldn't care less anyhow.

Chuck's the closest thing I have to family anymore. He thinks I should trust you. He says there's gotta be somebody somewhere who knows what to do. What he means is, somebody smarter than him. Someone who went to school and doesn't drink too much.

But I know what Kat would say. She's probably right, too. *Ain't nobody comin' to save you, girl. You wanna survive? You better start thinking for yourself. And if I was you, I wouldn't tell nobody nothing. Just fuckin' run.*

Trouble is, I got nowhere else to go. This is it. My big idea. My last chance before I'm back outside and he finds me. He knows what I did. If he finds me, he'll go crazy. Crazy enough to kill me, maybe, and then I can finally sleep.

"Michelle?" Your voice pulls me back into the room. "Try to stay with me, okay?"

I got no way to prove who I am. I got no ID, no Social Security card. I grew up in Philly on North 26th Street, but I know nobody's there anymore, so there's no point telling you that. All I got is this busted-up face and the stupid hope that maybe Chuck's right. Somebody's gotta know what to do. And if you don't, at least you'll know my name. My real name. You'll know I was here before he got me, and that I wasn't always like this.

You lean forward and reach for my face. At first I flinch, waiting for a punch or a push or something else that hurts. Then you brush a tattered braid from my eyes and rest your hand on mine.

"Who did this to you, Michelle?"

I close my eyes and pretend your hand is his.

Two months ago, something incredible happened. I got rescued by a guy. He found me in the middle of the bus station on the day I prayed for a miracle. He had long, strong arms and a clean black car and new clothes that smelled like soap.

And he took my face in his hands and looked right into me and said, "I'm gonna take care of you, 'Chelle. I swear."

"Michelle?" you say, a bit louder. "Do you know who did this?"

The door opens. Two nurses stand over me.

"I'm sorry," one of them says in a voice with sharp edges. "We need to get her upstairs."

I reach out, handing you the crumpled card with your name on it.

"Please," the nurse insists. "We need to get moving."

You stare at the card, then search my face. "Have we met before? Wait, please. Just a minute. Michelle? Who did this to you?"

"My daddy," I whisper, trying to keep my voice steady.

"Your father?"

I shake my head no and I lock my eyes with yours. Then I pull down my gown and point to my tattoo, his name sunk deep into my chest, the orange peach above it.

"My daddy."

I keep pointing until your eyes widen and you finally nod and sigh and say, "Okay." I sigh too because I think you remember who I am. And I think maybe you understand what I mean.

STRAWBERRY MANSION

Northwest Philadelphia

I am five years old. The TV glows all soft and bluish in my toasty-warm living room. It's winter. My house smells like meat loaf and corn. The windows are shut tight, but I can hear the noises outside. Cars and voices and music going by. Chuck and Little John laughing in their lawn chairs outside Boo's.

Grandpa's on our brown smushy couch. That's where he sleeps. His clothes are folded in a pile in the corner. Dirty clothes go in the plastic bag. Clean clothes get folded in the pile.

Grandpa grins and pats the couch. "C'mere, Punky."

I run over and climb into his lap. I pull red bear blanket over my head so it's all dark and warm and I can't see anything. I am in a cave. A secret cave. Grandpa's heart goes *thump, thump, thump.* Like he's a big, friendly bear that lets me share his secret hideout. I close my eyes and curl up my legs and smush myself all tight inside.

Grandpa strokes my head and watches the newsman on TV. It's gonna snow tomorrow. Snow in Philadelphia! Outside music bangs from a car passing by. Quiet again, then a siren whistles a few blocks away. Grandpa turns up the volume a little, hums, and puts his chin on my head.

My belly is full. Meat loaf and corn! My pajama pants are red stripes, and Grandpa's big gray T-shirt that he sometimes lets me sleep in.

"Ready for bed?" Grandpa's voice is big. His giant chest rumbles when he talks. *Thump thump. Hum. Hum. Hummm.*

"One more minute." I shove my thumb into my mouth.

I can feel his face smile on my head. *Click*. The TV's off and he pats my arm. "School tomorrow. Remember."

"One more minute."

Grandpa grabs my waist and lifts me over his shoulder. "Off to bed, little girl!" he growls. I laugh and kick and *bounce bounce bounce* we go up the stairs.

He takes my hand and we walk down the hall to my bedroom, past Mama's door. It's open. Her bed is messy. Clothes on the floor. A strange smell, like fire and plastic. She's not home.

"Where's Mama?" I ask. Grandpa sits on the floor next to my mattress and pulls my blanket up around my neck.

"Just out," he says. "Close your eyes. Time to sleep."

"Where?"

He kisses my forehead. His hair is short and black with little bits of white mixed in. His skin is brown. He has lines in his forehead and six black dots under his eye. They look like chocolate chips. Like a giant cookie face with white hair sprinkles.

"She'll be back. Time to sleep, Punky. Wanna read a book?"

I shrug and smush my face into the pillow.

Grandpa finds yellow bunny in the corner. I hold her tight and put my thumb in my mouth.

"Let's read George. George and the Dump Truck."

George is a monkey. He gets into trouble a lot, but he doesn't mean to and nobody ever gets mad at him.

Grandpa opens the book. I close my eyes and feel my thumb all warm and soft. Bunny under red bear blanket. Meat loaf and corn. Outside I hear Chuck and Little John. They laugh. Tomorrow it will snow.

Grandpa reads.

This is George. He was a good little monkey and always very curious.

I'm seven years old.

It's cold, but my house smells warm. Chicken and green beans. I can cook the cutlets by myself now. Dip the chicken in eggs. Then bread crumbs. Put them in the pan with butter. Don't leave them too long or they'll get dry. Save the extra eggs for breakfast.

Chuck and Little John wave to me from their chairs outside Boo's Lounge. I open the window and cold air nibbles at my face.

"You bein' good, Michelle?" Chuck shouts. "Santa

ain't comin' if you bad. You better do your homework, little girl."

I grin and yell back, "I ain't bad! I'm a GOOD girl!" and they all laugh and nod and Little John knocks over his brown paper bag with the bottle in it. Chuck laughs harder. Me too.

Grandpa smiles. "C'mon, Punks. Time for bed. And don't say *ain't*."

"Chuck says ain't."

"Exactly."

"So does Mama."

Grandpa pauses on the stairs, then keeps walking, past her broken door that's mostly closed.

"Just don't say it, Punks. You talk poor, you stay poor."

On the floor by my mattress, after our book, he makes me practice:

"What do you do if you're lost or in trouble?"

I groan, but I know he won't leave till I finish.

"Look for a cop," I grumble.

"Speak up."

"I look for a cop in a uniform," I say a little louder.

"But what if you can't find one?"

"A lady. I look for a lady."

"Why do we look for a lady?"

"'Cause ladies like to help little kids."

Grandpa smiles down at me. "Good girl," he whispers. "Good girl."

Morning.

Mama piled on the couch like laundry.

Grandpa rushes in the kitchen.

Wake. Dress. Breakfast. Cereal today. Don't leave flakes in the drain or the bugs will come back, creeping through the cracks from the house next door where nobody lives and it stinks.

I can smell the snow outside. I peek through the living room window at the clean white snow cushions on the chairs outside Boo's.

"Let's go, Punks. We're late. Where's your hat?"

"In my pocket."

"Put it on. It's freezing out."

He looks at her. "Your mom'll be here when you get home, all right?"

She's staring at the TV, her eyes all red and slow and gone.

"Corinna!" Grandpa shouts. Mama rolls her eyes and shuffles over, fiddles with my coat even though I'm all zipped up.

"Look at this child," she mumbles, grabbing a chunk of hair that sticks out from under my hat. "Hold on." Mama goes upstairs for a minute, then comes back with a white barrette, a rubber band, and a comb. She pulls my hat off and fixes my hair in a ponytail. The teeth of the barrette dig into my scalp. She pushes hard, harder, till it clicks.

"That's better," she says.

My arms around her waist. Too tight.

"I'm gonna draw you a picture today," I say into her floppy shirt, and squeeze like it's red bear blanket over my head.

She'll be awake when I get home. I'll make us a snack like peanut butter toast and be good so she doesn't get bored and fall asleep.

Grandpa opens the front door. His bear head hangs as frozen air runs inside our house.

Mama shivers and lets me go.

3

CONEY ISLAND HOSPITAL

Coney Island, New York

I know he's a cop the second I open my eye. He's short and thick, with blue eyes and a shaved face, his hair buzzed short like a soldier. There's a gun on his hip, black and huge.

He talks loud, his words hammering at my sore head. "Hey! You awake?"

My right eye won't open at all. My left, only a little. I shut it tight, praying he didn't see me move.

"Hey," he says again. "Time to get up."

The lights blast on above my bed, the whiteness screaming at my fat eyelids.

Don't move. Stay still. Just breathe real slow and he'll think you're still asleep.

Where are you, Daniela Cespedes, CSW?

Click. The mattress groans to life beneath me, pushing me upright. I peek out from my bandages. He's holding a large remote in his hand, making the bed move. There's a second cop now—a woman—standing by the window. Watching me.

"Hey," he says a little softer. "It's okay."

My heart bangs underneath the skin-thin hospital blankets, blood shooting to my cheeks, my raw gums, my lips that feel like ground-up bloodred meat, down into my stomach like a sick stew.

"My name's Mike. I'm a detective. Where you from, kiddo?"

He doesn't know anything. He doesn't know what I am. He can't arrest me. I'm too young, like Kat said. Just stay still. He'll go away.

"Michelle?" he says. My eye opens.

"Aha! So we know that's your name. So. Michelle. Let's start simple. Where's your mother?"

I want to lie flat again. I want to go to sleep. I want my face to stop hurting. I want you to come back.

My stomach starts to boil. It burns and churns up into my throat.

Then you step into the thin strip of what I can actually see.

"I think that's enough for now," you say to him. "You can come back later. She's pretty beat up. She needs to rest."

"We got a schedule too," the girl cop snaps.

You don't say anything back, just sort of stand there and sigh and rub your forehead like you're as tired as I am.

"She's dead." The words creak out of me, my sore lips cracking as I form each letter.

"What?" The cop leans over me, his gun tapping against the metal railing of my bed.

"My mother's dead," I repeat, and vomit leaks out of my mouth.

4

STRAWBERRY MANSION

North Philadelphia

I'm nine.

It's late at night and I can't fall asleep, so I look outside my window. Voices and cars and music passing by.
It's almost spring. The mounds of old snow, covered in
dirt like hard black frosting, are almost gone.

Grandpa's in front of Boo's Lounge with Chuck and
Little John and other men who only come at night.
Chuck says something to Grandpa, then laughs so hard
he starts coughing and has to take a sip from his bottle.

Grandpa pats his back with a smile. Chuck's a mess, Grandpa says, but we love him anyway.

Then I see her. Walking with her head down. Her hair's all frizzy and she moves all slow, like her body hurts. Chuck and Little John get quiet.

She hasn't been home in five nights.

Suddenly, Grandpa's across the street. He takes her by the shoulders and lifts her chin with his finger and makes Mama look at him. He examines her, then shoves his hands into her pockets. She pushes him away and I hear the creak of the front door, her feet dragging slowly up the stairs.

"Mama?" I say into the dark. Her ghost-body floats down the hall, stopping for a second to look at me in my doorway. I wait for her to say, *Go back to sleep, baby.* Or, *It's late, 'Chelle. Why ain't you in bed?*

But she doesn't say anything. She just closes the door behind her.

She'll be sleeping when I go to school tomorrow. She'll be gone when I get home. She's gonna eat the chicken too, and then we won't have nothin' for dinner.

Anything.

I think she's a junkie. Like the man in the blue house

with the saggy roof up the block that Grandpa says I gotta stay away from. He got nasty scabs on his face, like the ones on Mama's arms.

I think she's like the people who visit the boys on the corner up from Boo's, late at night when I'm supposed to be asleep.

Junkies.

Like Erica's mom. We seen her once, last spring, outside Sun Moon Chinese after school. Just standing there on the corner, her hair all crazy, her stomach spilling out of her too-small shorts. She called to us. *Erica! Hold up, baby!* But Erica grabbed my hand and we ran. I never seen Erica run in all my life, but that day we ran so fast I thought my chest was gonna explode when we finally stopped, like, ten blocks away.

"Why we runnin', E?" I panted. But she just shook her head and looked away from me, her eyes all wet like she was gonna cry, which was even crazier than seeing her run, 'cause Erica doesn't cry. Not ever. But that day, she almost did.

Erica got a new family now. A foster family with a mom and a dad and a couple other kids too. I told her it was good because she's my friend and I love her and maybe her new mom will do her hair up like the other girls at school. But it's been six months and Erica don't look any different. Except her eyes. They got hard, like cement.

"I got a door on my room," she said when I asked her what her new house was like. Then she folded her arms up like she does now, like she wished they could make her disappear.

"I don't like it there," she whispered.

"How come?"

"I just don't." She shrugged and stared at the cold cafeteria floor.

I grab my yellow bunny and curl up tiny and tight beneath my blanket.

I am in a cave.

Morning.

I don't wanna go to school.

I tell Grandpa I don't feel good, but he puts his giant hand on my forehead.

"You don't have a fever, Punks. You gotta go."

I don't say another word, just grab my backpack and pretend to walk to school before circling back to the house. I check to make sure Grandpa's gone, and then I let myself in.

I climb the stairs, dump my bag on the floor. Then I start in the bathroom. Bucket, Pine-Sol, hot water, and the towel we keep just for cleaning. I wipe everything, even the floor, then go downstairs and wipe down the kitchen again, even though we do that every morning anyway. I make a peanut butter sandwich, wrap it up tight in plastic wrap, and leave it on the counter with a note that says, *For you, Mama. Love, Michelle.*

I lie on my bed and wait for her. Wait to hear the door open till I can't help it and my eyes close.

When I wake up, someone's in the shower. The TV's on downstairs.

Mom is on the couch in panties and a tank top. She's lying down sort of sideways, her head arched back on her skinny neck like she's frozen in place. Her fingers are curled, her hands out in front of her like they're floating. I go over and cover her with a blanket.

Her eyes. I don't know what she's looking at. The ceiling?

What's wrong with her?

Who's in the shower?

"Mom?" The sandwich is still on the kitchen table.

She drags her eyes toward me. "'Chelle?" she murmurs—slow, sloppy—and her mouth turns up into a smile. "Baby? How'd you get here? C'mere and sit with your mama."

She lies all the way down, her arms open like paper-thin curtains. I go to her. I climb right beside her and let them close behind me, smushed together on the couch, my nose in her neck.

"Are you okay?"

"Mmm-hmmm . . . ," she murmurs.

"I cleaned the house. I made you a sandwich," I say.

Her breath is deep, long and hard like she's sleeping, but her eyes are still sort of open. She's so warm. I try not to look down at her bare legs, scabby and marked and grayish. My beautiful mama, all torn up.

"You my baby," she says, over and over, and she hugs me like I'm yellow bunny. "My baby. My baby." I squeeze her so hard, I bury my face so hard into her, I want to climb inside so she can see. So she can see that I am good and so is Grandpa and she can stay with us and she don't need to be so dirty like those other people.

She ain't like that, my mom. Not mine. Not you, Mama.

"Don't go away no more," I say.

"Mmmm," she says.

The shower turns off upstairs.

"Who's here?" I ask.

Her arms go soft at her sides. She's asleep.

A man walks down the stairs with one of Grandpa's towels wrapped around his waist. He is tall with wide shoulders and a long, thin face. I don't know who he is. He looks at us, his face sort of split in half, his mouth smiling, his eyes not.

"What'chu doin' home, little girl?" he says.

"Mama," I whisper, nudging her.

The man steps closer. "You Corinna's kid?" I nod. I want to get under the blanket. "Yeah. You look like her. How old are you?"

I do not answer. He stares at me. I stare back.

"Don't be scared," he says, laughing. "I'm your mama's friend."

"I don't know you," I say.

He strolls into the kitchen and looks at the sandwich I made. He reads the card too.

"That's sweet," he says. Then he strolls back and puts

his hand on my face. On my cheek.

I pull away. *What do you do if you're in trouble?*

Find a lady.

"Mom!" I say, but loud. Really loud. Right in her face. I push her chest a little. She jiggles, then jerks, her eyes slide open for a second, then roll back into sleep.

"She's gonna wake up and make you leave," I say to him.

"Oh yeah? Stand up."

"No," I say.

"Stand up." And I do. I stand. Because Mama won't get up and Grandpa's not here and I'm supposed to be in school but I didn't go and I've never done that before and what if I scream and the cops come and Grandpa gets mad and makes her leave forever.

He leans over, the towel dangling in front of him, and puts his face right up to mine.

"Wake up, Corinna," he whispers in a little girl's voice. "Wake up."

He grabs my bottom, his fingers dig in hard, almost lifting me off the floor. He lets go and I stagger back into Mama, whose limp arm dangles. Useless. Then he walks to the kitchen and bites into the peanut butter sandwich.

"Go upstairs," he says. "And keep your mouth shut or I'll tell your grandpa you been skippin' school."

I run to the stairs. Go. Go. Get to your room. Close the door.

But even in here, it feels like his hand is still on me.

5

CONEY ISLAND HOSPITAL

Coney Island, New York

You ask me if I'm all right, but I won't answer. My room stinks like puke, even though they changed my sheets and cleaned the floor. The cops are still here, outside in the hall, waiting for me.

"Michelle?"

I glare at you as best I can from my one working eye.

"You're angry," you say.

You're right.

"What did you tell them?" I ask.

"I told them what I knew."

You pause, like you're picking your words real careful. "I told them the truth: that your name is Michelle. You were beaten and we don't know more than that. I didn't tell them anything else. I'm not going to. Not until we talk, you and me, okay?"

"I can't see right."

"Your eyes are still swollen. They'll get better with time. So, what are we gonna do here, Michelle? You found me. I'm here. So, let's figure out our next move. The sooner you talk, the sooner we can do that, okay? Let's start with your mom. Did she really pass away?"

I shrug and turn away from you. Please. Just let me sleep.

"Michelle? Is your mother dead?"

I want to say yes. I want it to be true. I want to say she's the one who died on the couch last year, who got wheeled out on a stretcher and never came back. I want it to be her.

But the wrong people die. The dead people are the good ones, the bad ones get to walk around like nothing. Like they got a right to keep breathing while the ones you need just leave their skin, waste away till there ain't nothing left but a stupid dirty T-shirt and what you can barely remember.

"Yeah," I say. "She's dead."

Quiet. Your eyes settle on me. "Who else, then? Who else can we call?"

Grandpa. That's who you should call. He'd tell all of you to stay the hell away from me.

C'mon, Punks. Let's go home.

"What happens if there ain't nobody else?" I ask.

But I already know the answer.

Nothing good. Not for me. Not for any of us.

6

STRAWBERRY MANSION

North Philadelphia

I'm fourteen.

"Hey, Punky."

The words rattle out of Grandpa's mouth, more air than sound.

"Hey," I say, pulling up the blanket to his chin, over the empty space where his belly used to be. It's gone now. So is the fat in his cheeks. Like someone let the air out.

That's what tumors do. Like the one he's got in his stomach.

He stays on the couch all day now.

Tonight, Mama sits me on the floor and works hard on my hair, combing and pulling till it's tight in a ponytail. She pulls too hard, but I don't complain because Grandpa's eyes shimmer a little, like maybe this will all be okay. Like maybe he can leave and we'll be fine.

His hands. His hands are still big. Grandpa's bear paws.

Scoop me up, Grandpa. Pretend you are a bear. Throw me over your shoulder, carry me up the stairs, because it's late and I should be in bed. I still need somebody to take care of me.

Time for bed, Punks. School tomorrow. Remember.

I stay up late and watch him breathe, watch the up and down of his chest till I fall asleep on the floor next to him.

In the morning, he's still.

I go outside and sit on the step till I hear my mother shout. Then I know it's true.

Erica once told me there's pain so bad, your body won't let you feel it. Like if your leg gets cut off. Or if you're burned alive.

He's gone.

My grandpa.

Now it's just me and her.

Springtime.

I open the door to my room. Calvin is sprawled on my bed. His dirty fingers touch my red bear blanket.

The room is dark except for a dim yellow light from the window. I drop my book bag and turn to leave, but where? Suddenly he's up and in my face.

"Hey, girl," he whispers. "Where you been?"

Keep still. Don't move. Stop shaking.

His lips pull back into a smile. Yellow teeth and stinking breath and milky eyes pour over me. He touches my face with his fingers.

I pull away, but he just moves closer.

"What do you want?"

"I wanna see how you doing. I know it's been hard on you lately. With your grandpa gone."

I don't say anything.

"You know, my daddy died when I was your age. I know it ain't easy." He touches my face again, looks down toward my hips. "You ever wanna talk about it, maybe I can help, you know?"

"I'm good," I say.

He moves closer, his lips skid against my mouth. I clench my teeth and my legs turn to water. He holds my head still. His tongue on my lips.

Downstairs, people are talking and walking around. Someone passes my door, peers in, and keeps going.

I shake my head away. "Stop," I whimper. *Please.*

Calvin pushes up against me. "You miss your grandpa?"

He scratches his grimy black hair. Flecks of white fall on his shoulders. He's not wearing a shirt.

"Don't worry," he whispers. "I'm gonna look out for y'all. Understand?" Then his mouth's on me again, but harder this time, pushing past my teeth. I try to bite it, bite his tongue like a slug in my mouth. I push hard against his sticky skin, and it feels like I'm drowning and nothing works. My legs, my hands, my teeth, it's all sinking away from me and I can't stop him digging into my face. Stop it. Please.

"Yo, Calvin!" someone yells from the hall. "Corinna lookin' for you!"

He lets me go and wipes his mouth. I gasp, my heart

punching at my chest bone, and I picture Grandpa busting through the door, Calvin slamming to the ground as Grandpa growls in his face. Grandpa, gathering me up into his arms. Me, curling myself into his lap.

Then I see my mother in the doorway, her thin body like a shadow in the flimsy yellow light. She stares at us and scratches at her arm, her eyes all glassy and slow. She looks confused.

"What the fuck?" she murmurs.

Calvin wipes his mouth again. He glares at her, his eyes challenging and angry, as if he's daring her to speak. She lowers her head and looks at the floor. Then he chuckles, pats her bottom, and disappears into the hallway.

"Mama," I whisper.

She points her finger at the dark. "You tryin' to take him away from me? I see the way you been walkin' around here, all cute and shit."

She sways, wipes her nose. "Stay away from him. Hear me?"

Deep inside my chest, my heart jams up for a second and all the air goes out of me. Empty. Like Grandpa on the couch the night he died.

She turns away and shuts my door and then she's gone.

I push my bed against the door and crawl into the corner of my room. Through the floorboards, her words to Calvin slice the dark.

"C'mere, baby," she says, her voice soft and young. Like a little girl's. Calvin laughs again. I grab my book bag and hug it to my chest, Grandpa's words echoing in my head.

What do you do if you're in trouble?

Chuck tries to watch me. He sits in his chair outside Boo's and watches the house till he's too drunk to see it. He drinks more now that Grandpa's gone. I think I make him sad. After school he asks me questions like, who's coming over and do we have enough money? I smile and lie and say it's not that bad, because I don't want him calling the cops.

Find a cop.

They'll send me to a group home. Like that place on Broad and Olney where Erica went. The place she wouldn't talk about, even when she showed up at my house with a busted lip. I tried to ask her questions, to find out what it's like there, but she'd only shake her head and fold her arms tight across her chest. Then one night she showed up all bouncy, her eyes bright and secretive.

I'm leavin', 'Chelle. I'm goin' to New York. Me and my roommate. She got a cousin there.

Then she slipped me a crumpled piece of paper with an address scrawled in sloppy handwriting, like whoever wrote it didn't have much time.

Pink Houses
Crescent Street
New York

Pink houses. Were they really pink?
You should come visit, 'Chelle. Once I get all set up.
How you know it'll be better in New York? I'd asked.
Erica shrugged, her shoulders falling slightly.
Can't nothin' be worse than here, she'd said. A few days later, I tried to call her cell phone, but all I heard was the three long beeps you get when you don't have no more time left on your prepaid.

✍

Find a lady.

There is no magic lady. No one's gonna bring me home to Grandpa.

I pull up the carpet in the corner of my room and count the money from Grandpa's stash. Fifty-one dollars left. I used to have eighty-four dollars, but I gotta spend more now that school's out. It's June. By August, I won't have anything left.

I tuck the bills back under the rug and carefully push the carpet back into place. Then I curl up on the floor below the window.

For a long time I lay in the dark until my eyes grow heavy and I drift off into a fitful sleep. I think I hear someone calling me. Shouting, a siren squealing past, the *thump thump thump* of music. Something shatters.

Then I hear the sound of heavy footsteps. The doorknob turns slightly.

Tap. Tap. Tap. "I know you in there."

Calvin's voice grabs at me through the door. I crawl into my closet and wait until his shadow walks away. He can't get in—not tonight, not with the bed against the door. But someday he will. I know it.

❧

What do you do if you're in trouble?

I wait for the answer to come to me. But there's only darkness and Calvin's voice and my own heart, pounding like feet on the pavement, running away, running away, running away.

Morning.

My mother's sitting in the kitchen. She's smoking a cigarette and drinking coffee, a crumpled paper bag on the table before her.

"You can't stay here no more," she says. "I'm sorry, 'Chelle, but you can't."

"What?"

"You heard me. Don't play dumb."

"It ain't my fault," I say. "He was there when I got home."

"I know. It don't matter."

Mom drops her cigarette into her coffee. It hisses as it hits the brown liquid, a trail of smoke rising in the still air.

"I know I ain't right," she continues. Her voice wobbles as she stares at the table, her eyes like liquid, like they're about to spill out onto the floor. "I know I ain't. But me and Calvin . . ." For a moment, she looks like the girl in the photo from when I was a baby, her eyes far away and sad.

"You got friends, Michelle? Good friends?"

I shiver.

Mom slides the bag across the table to me. "There's forty dollars in there, and the WIC card for this month so you can get food. You go stay with one of your friends. Someone good. You let me know when you all set up, okay?"

She stands up and heads for the stairs, her bare feet scraping on the floor. Rage swells up in me, tears out of me toward her, and I push. I push so fucking hard I knock her to the ground. Then I grab the paper bag and throw it at her crumpled body.

"I don't need shit from you," I spit.

She pulls herself up and shuffles to the stairs.

"You're gonna miss me," I hiss. "You don't know."

Her foot on the step.

"Ain't you even gonna ask me where I'm going?"

She stops. Turns. "Can't nothin' be worse than here," she says. "You smart, Michelle." And then, "Not like me."

Her thin body struggles, step by dirty step. A door closes softly. A lighter clicks, and then the smell of smoke.

What do you do if you're in trouble?

I got fifty-one dollars and an address.

Pink Houses.

That's where I will go.

1

GREYHOUND BUS TERMINAL

10th and Filbert Streets, Philadelphia

The bus station's crammed with every possible kind of person, rushing and standing and waiting in lines. A woman with shiny blond hair and tight dark blue jeans talks on her cell phone and sips a cup of coffee with whipped cream on top. A guy with a huge duffel bag and red sweatshirt that says UPENN dashes to the line at the ticket counter. A mother pushes a sleeping baby in a stroller. An old woman sits in a wheelchair by the door, dozing off under a blanket.

My heart pumps hard. It's nine thirty a.m. Overhead, a giant schedule flashes the names of places I've never been to.

> *Atlantic City, New Jersey 9:45 a.m.*
> *New York City 10:00 a.m.*
> *Norfolk, Virginia 10:30 a.m.*
> *Boston 11:15 a.m.*

I hug my pillow and step into line behind the boy in the sweatshirt.

"Next!" yells the woman behind the counter. The boy steps up, flips open his wallet, pulls out a credit card, and taps it absentmindedly on the counter.

"Round trip to Boston," he says. She types something into her computer.

"A hundred twenty-nine fifty," she replies without looking up. My face flushes and I grab my pillow tighter. I don't have that kind of money. What if a ticket to New York costs more than what I got?

The boy swipes his card, signs his name, takes his ticket, and strides off into the crowd.

"Next!" she calls. I clench my fifty-one dollars in my

hand. Above my head, the names of cities scroll by.

> *Toronto, Canada 9:50 a.m.*
> *Columbus, Ohio 11:45 a.m.*
> *Orlando, Florida 12:00 p.m.*

"Next!" she repeats, raising her eyebrow at me.

I glance behind me. There's a long line of people. An older woman in a big red hat puts her hand on my shoulder.

"Your turn," she says gently. Her face is soft, and she's wearing red lipstick that leaks into the wrinkles around her mouth.

"You can go," I say, trying to sound casual. My hands start to sweat, soaking the money in my tight fist.

"You sure?" she says. "Do you need help?"

"Yeah." I nod and force myself to smile. "I mean, no. You can go 'head."

She smiles and walks to the counter.

"One way to New York," she says.

"Forty-three seventy-five."

One way to New York. Only forty-three dollars. I glance around, almost expecting to see the cops or

Calvin or my mother coming for me. But nobody's there. Just strangers.

The woman swipes her card and steps aside, smiling at me. She must have kids, the way her eyes get soft like she wants to make sure I'm okay. I smile and sigh. My heart slows down a little.

"Your turn," she chirps.

"C'mon!" someone shouts behind me.

I step up to the counter. "One way to New York," I say carefully, trying to sound like I've done this before.

"That's forty-three dollars and seventy-five cents."

I hand her my damp, wrinkled bills. She watches me, then types into the computer and hands me a ticket.

I follow the woman in the red hat outside to where the buses are lined up on the street. Their engines roar and spew black smoke into the air. Someone bumps my shoulder, sending my pillow into a dirty puddle.

"Hey!" yells the woman in the red hat. "Watch it!"

My pillow's soaked. So is red bear blanket, stuffed inside the pillowcase.

"You okay?" she asks me.

I shrug and stare at the ground, suddenly wishing I was back in my house in my closet. I didn't say good-bye to Chuck. I should've brought my pajamas. I cannot cry. Not in front of this woman, who might realize I'm running away and turn me in.

"You here by yourself?"

"Nah," I lie. "My grandpa—he dropped me off. I'm going to see my mom."

"You goin' all the way to New York by yourself?"

"She's gonna meet me there. Where the bus drops us off."

Her forehead wrinkles. "At Port Authority?"

"Yeah. Port Authority."

She sighs. "How 'bout we sit together?"

I hesitate.

"C'mon," she says with a smile, reaching out a hand to me. Her nails are red and neat, like her hat and her lipstick and her clean coat. "You can tell me all about your mom. I'm Betty, by the way."

"Sarah," I reply, and step onto the huge coughing bus.

For three hours, I find myself talking to Betty. I can't stop the words from tumbling out of my mouth. My grandpa's a doctor, I tell her, a cancer doctor. I'm going to stay with my mom. She's an actress. In New York City. She's pretty and she can't wait to see me. Betty nods and doesn't say much. When she pulls out a bagel from her bag, my stomach growls so loudly that she gives me half. I devour it, licking the cream cheese from my fingers, and keep talking. I'm going to be an actress when I'm older, just like my mom. Someday I'll be pretty too.

"It must be hard, living so far away from her," Betty says, handing me a paper napkin.

"Yeah," I say. "She misses me all the time."

The New York skyline grows larger and larger in the window, the buildings like strangers standing in line, waiting for me to get there. We plunge into a long, dark tunnel and then we're surrounded by skyscrapers. They go on for blocks. We inch along slowly, crawling down a wide street clogged up with cars and taxis and bicycles and people swarming the sidewalks.

The bus hisses to a stop in a huge underground garage. My heart hurries. New York City. They make movies here.

In the bus terminal, me and Betty glide up an escalator. Hundreds of people flow by, an ocean of strangers.

There are stores and restaurants, the smell of food everywhere, and subways rumbling deep underground.

Betty grips my arm tightly. "Let's find this mother of yours," she says, but her voice sounds different. Harder.

"She's probably late anyway. I'll just wait for her here. Thanks. For everything. Really." I try to pull my hand away, but Betty won't let go.

"Why don't I wait with you?" she says, and her eyes look right into me. My hands start to sweat. Two police-men stand by the front doors. She glances at them, then back at me. There's someone else too. A guy in a crisp white T-shirt and dark blue jeans. He's watching us. He smiles and nods his head, like he knows who I am. Like he's waiting for me. Our eyes meet and though I'm not sure why, I smile back.

"Who's that?" Betty asks in a firm voice.

"I'm sorry," I say, yanking my hand away.

"Wait! Sarah!" she yells, but I'm already gone, running through the crowd, past stores and benches and people racing to work or home or to families that miss them. It's not hard to disappear here, with so many people.

I duck into a store and hide between the racks of

shirts and stuffed animals. I throw on my hoodie and keep my head down. After ten minutes, I walk back out into the main terminal. Betty's still there, talking to the cops. I turn back to the store, but the woman behind the counter glares at me.

"Can I help you?" she snaps.

I take a deep breath and fish out Erica's address from my backpack.

"Do you know how to get here?" I say.

The woman looks at the address. "This in the city?"

"What?"

"Is this in the city?"

"Yeah. In New York."

She hands the address back to me. "I never heard of Crescent Street. Maybe it's in Queens. Or the Bronx. You gonna buy something?"

"Nah. Thank you," I say, and I step back out into the main terminal.

And then he's there again, the guy in the white T-shirt, leaning against the wall with a toothpick in his mouth.

"You shouldn't run," he says in a low voice, as if we're

sharing a secret. "You'll draw attention to yourself. The cops are lookin' for you now."

"I'm meeting my uncle," I say quickly.

His mouth curls up into a knowing smile. "Then why you runnin'?"

I shrug and clutch my filthy pillow. His teeth are bright white, and he smells like soap and french fries. A thin silver chain hangs from his neck.

"C'mon. I'll get you outta here," he continues.

"Nah," I say weakly. "I'm good."

He raises an eyebrow. "You don't look so good."

I glance down at my dirty blue T-shirt and baggy jeans. My sneakers are ripped and faded. I run my hand through my hair and pull at the front of my shirt nervously. His sneakers are out-the-box red. Not a speck of dirt on them. His hair is cut short, buzzed into a neat curving hairline around his dark, sharp face. His skin shines, waxy like a car.

"You hungry?" he asks. I don't answer, even though my stomach rumbles. He tosses his toothpick on the floor, shrugs, and turns to leave.

"I wouldn't go out the front door if I was you," he says. "Good luck, girl. If you want a burger, I'll be at

McDonald's over there for a half hour."

Then he disappears into the crowd.

I don't know where to go. I walk along the wall and keep my head down. A woman in a loose flowery shirt and red skirt that flips back and forth brushes by me. She looks like she knows where she's going, so I follow her. Down a set of stairs, then across a platform and down more stairs. She swipes a card and pushes through a turnstile and then she's gone too.

The subway.

The signs don't make sense. ACE with blue circles. Downtown. Red circles with the numbers 1, 2, and 3. Crosstown. NR in yellow circles. Queens. There's a big map on the dirty tiled wall, covered with different-colored curvy lines and a million tiny street names. More numbers, more colors. I search for Crescent Street, for the color pink. A man walks up and checks the map, tracing one of the blue lines with his finger. He's wearing a suit and shiny black shoes. I pull my hood back, stand up straight, and smile.

"Do you know where Crescent Street is?"

"Crescent? Sounds like it's in the Village. Maybe ask

that guy." He points to a man in a booth by the turn-stiles and hurries off.

I approach the thick glass, suddenly wishing I was back home buying gummy worms at the corner store. I press the address on the glass. The man looks at it, then at me, and shakes his head. "You got a cross street?"

No, I don't have a cross strect. I don't know what that means. I pull my hood up and walk away fast, past the map that doesn't make sense, past the people who just keep coming and coming and coming, shoving my shoulders, looking through me for the trains that will take them where they belong. The subways squeal, *ding-dong* as the doors close, and rattle off slowly while others tear by so fast they make me dizzy.

My head slams with pain. I'm hungry and thirsty and tired and I don't know to find Pink Houses. I only have seven dollars left. I climb back up the stairs, pushing against thc crowd, and walk to McDonald's.

He's sitting in a booth in the corner, checking his phone. There are two trays on the table. Two full meals. He smiles when he sees me, his eyes like open doors.

"There you are," he says. "I was hopin' you'd come back. Sit. Eat."

I slide into the booth across from him and ball my hands into fists so he won't see them shaking. I can smell the salt from the french fries, the burger warm and wrapped up, waiting for me.

"Thanks," I whisper.

"No problem." He nods.

I eat in silence, trying to control myself as I suck down the soda, bite the salty fries, sink my teeth into the fat burger, blobs of ketchup plopping on the tray. I wipe my mouth with a napkin and fold it, nervously, in my hands. A wave of exhaustion crashes over me. I want to keep eating. I want to sleep. But the food's gone and I have no bed.

"You want more?" he asks.

"Nah, thanks," I lie. I slide the address across the table. "You know where this is?"

He looks at the paper. Something shifts in his face. He sits up straight. "You jokin', right?"

"What?"

He looks me over. "Who you know at Pink?"

"You know how to get there?! My friend Erica. Erica

Davis," I answer. "That's where she lives. I gotta get there. I gotta find her."

He watches me, then looks at the address again. "What building she in?"

"I don't know. Can you tell me how to get there? Can I take the subway? I got money. I got—"

"Subways don't run that far out. Pink's way down by the Belt. You could take a cab maybe, but that's gonna cost you, like, fifty bucks."

I look at him. "I gotta get there. You don't understand."

He is still, silent in his clean shirt, the empty trays of food between us. In the booth behind him, a little girl smiles at me.

"Please," I say.

He sighs. "All right. I'll take you there myself. You don't want to be gettin' lost in Pink. You got any cash?"

"Take it," I gasp, sliding my last seven dollars across the table. "Thank you."

"You talkin' too loud." He glances around us, sliding the money into his pocket. He stands and holds out a hand to me. I grab my bag and pillow and jump up, almost knocking over my half-empty soda.

"Calm down."

"Sorry! It's just . . . thank you. Thank you."

He takes my backpack and slings it over his shoulder. "Don't get too excited. Pink's a big place, and you ain't got an apartment number. Can't you just call your friend?"

"Her phone don't work."

"Well, I ain't makin' no promises."

But I don't care. He knows the Pink Houses. I can find her. I just need to get there.

"What's your name?"

"Michelle," I say.

"I'm Devon. Put your hood down. And smile. Anybody asks, I'm your cousin, all right? Here we go." He takes my hand and leads me through the terminal, up a staircase, out a door, and into the street. It's bright and loud and there's noise everywhere, so I keep my head down and follow him to a glossy black car. He holds the door for me. I sink into the soft leather seats, smiling 'cause I can't believe it. I wonder if Grandpa can see me. If maybe he sent Devon to make sure I could get away.

I'm okay. See?

The car purrs to life. It smells like vanilla. Like a

cookie. Devon slips on a red baseball hat and a pair of sunglasses and pulls into the street, gliding between the million cars that swarm around us.

"You got any family?" he asks as we approach a huge bridge.

"Nah," I answer. Devon steers and nods to the music and smiles to himself, like he's as happy as I am. Like he knows exactly where he's taking me.

8

PINK HOUSES

Crescent Street and Linden Boulevard
Brooklyn, East New York

"Here you go," Devon says. "Pink Houses."

Four huge apartment buildings rise from the cement toward the fading orange sky—eight stories each of dirt-colored brick and small bar-covered windows cracked open to the warm air. Some have wet laundry half hanging out; others are blocked by noisy, dripping air conditioners that sag dangerously, as if they're exhausted, on the verge of giving up. In the courtyard there's a rusty playground, patches of half-dead grass, and two cement dolphins half-covered in flaking pink paint, with a warped metal sign in the middle of it all:

WELCOME TO LOUIS PINK HOUSES
A WONDERFUL COMMUNITY

Two young girls run past us, pushing a squeaky shopping cart filled with half-crushed boxes and a baby doll. Three guys stand by the dented metal door of a building marked 1. They nod in our direction. Devon nods back. One of them hollers loudly at us—a sound like a wolf—and Devon hollers back, tipping the rim of his red baseball hat.

"I don't understand," I say, staring up at the buildings. People are watching us. A man peers out from a third-floor window and blows smoke into the coming night. A mother on the second floor of a building marked 3 bounces a baby on her knee, its small hands reaching out from the metal bars. "What is this place?"

"The projects," he says, his arms open wide like he's inviting me into his home. "I grew up a couple blocks over, in Cypress. Pink's no joke, though. Must be a couple thousand apartments here."

"But there's only four buildings," I say.

Devon points toward the sinking sun. "Look over there. And there. And down Hemlock Ave."

The buildings don't stop. Beyond the courtyard, across another busy street, to my left, to my right, reaching up and out into the darkening sky, there are more and more buildings. Mud-colored brick buildings. Seven. Ten. Fifteen. On and on. I press my face to my pillow. I want to be back in my room.

The man at the window tosses his cigarette. It sparks like a tiny bomb when it hits the ground.

I feel so stupid. I pictured something beautiful, something pink and clean and safe. This is just another hood. Like Strawberry Mansion but with buildings, not houses.

"Unless you got an apartment number," Devon continues, "I don't think you're gonna find your girl."

"Maybe we could ask somebody. Someone in charge?"

"All right." Devon strides across the patchy grass toward the group of men outside Building 1. Two of the guys walk over to meet him, one short with droopy eyes and a red T-shirt, the other one taller, a baggy white T-shirt tucked into his sagging jean shorts. They tap fists and look in my direction. He waves me over.

"She's lookin' for her friend," Devon explains in a low voice. "She came down from—where you from?"

"Philly," I say, stepping closer. "Her name's Erica. She moved here a couple months ago."

"You got a picture?" says the short one with droopy eyes.

"Nah," I answer. "She's fourteen. Kinda heavy."

He shrugs at Devon. "No idea."

Someone's gotta know where she is. She gave me this address. She told me I should come here. She wants to see me.

Devon's car keys jingle in his hands. "So, what now?"

I don't know.

"Look. This place got a couple thousand people living in it. You don't even know what building she's in."

I cover my ears. I don't want to hear this. The smell of dinners being cooked and strangers walking and music creeping out of places I can't see; the little girls run by again, the shopping cart squealing like a tortured animal. My legs shift beneath me, threatening to cave in.

Devon puts his arm around my shoulder. "Easy, girl,"

he whispers. "Easy."

I push him away. What am I gonna do now? I can't go home. Even if I wanted to, all my money's gone and Mom don't want me there anyway. I don't even know how to get back to the bus station. I don't think we're in the city anymore. I don't know where we are. I don't know anything.

"It's all right," he whispers.

"No, it ain't," I snap. "You don't understand."

"Yeah, I do." He turns me toward him and lifts my chin with his finger. "You all alone. You got nobody. You got no place to go. You thought you'd find your girl here, but you can't. You scared and you don't know what to do."

His words pour into me like a secret. "Listen. Don't you think it's kinda crazy that I found you today? That I knew where this place was? Don't that seem strange to you? Like maybe we was supposed to meet. Like maybe I'm supposed to look out for you, 'cause I been where you are."

I wipe my nose with my hand and look up at him. He's right: it's crazy that he found me, it's crazy that he drove me all this way. He don't even know me. My own mother don't want me, but here he is, helping me out. He steps closer and puts his arm around my shoulder.

I freeze for a second. He's a big guy, bigger than Calvin. Big like Grandpa. He smells like soap and vanilla. Like laundry and clean socks. I feel a kiss on my forehead, warm and friendly. Safe.

'Night, Punky.

I lean into him.

"You can crash at my place tonight, all right? Me and my roommates—Kat and Baby. You'll be safe there. You can borrow some of their clothes if you need 'em."

Safe. Inside.

"Ain't none of us got family," he continues, gripping my hand like I might blow away, like I'm something important he won't let go. "So we make our own. C'mon. Let's get up outta here."

He leads me back to his car and I glance, once more, at Pink Houses—the place I came all this way to find. An older woman with her head wrapped in a scarf hurries by the guys who still stand outside Building 1. She lowers her head as she passes them, the metal doors slamming her inside. I shiver until Devon takes my face again and looks inside my sore, salty eyes.

"I got you, all right? I'm gonna take care of you, 'Chelle. I swear."

We drive onto a parkway that runs along the water, the jagged New York skyline smaller and smaller in the distance—like a picture of a city, not the real thing. Devon hums and leans away from me while the car glides along and finally exits where a green sign says SURF AVENUE, CONEY ISLAND. A block later, we stop alongside a large subway station with trains rattling on overhead tracks. A large crowd of passengers crosses the street in front of us, then we turn right onto a wide four-lane road. On the left side of the street, behind a flimsy chain-link fence, is a tremendous Ferris wheel, turning like a fluorescent moon.

I sit up.

The entire block is full of rides: small ones for little kids with boats and trucks for them to ride in, and bigger ones, too, like bumper cars. Across the street, at a window underneath a yellow-and-green sign that says NATHAN'S FAMOUS HOT DOGS, a line of customers wait to get food. Moms with kids. Couples. A group of girls, probably my age.

Where is Erica? Does she come here with her cousin?

The air is busy with smells: hot dogs, salt, sweet crispy dough. And something else.

The ocean.

"Are we near the beach?" I ask.

"Yeah." Devon smiles at me. "Back in the day this used to be the spot right here."

Five blocks later, the noise and lights are gone and the streets look like home: deserted except for the boys outside a bodega on the corner. Devon pulls into the parking lot of a tall apartment building, even bigger than the ones at Pink Houses.

"Lemme carry some of this shit for you." He takes my bag, and I hurry behind him through a heavy black door. The lobby walls are dirty yellow tile. There's an elevator, but he walks right past it and we climb up seven flights of steep cement stairs and sticky hot air that smells like pee and smoke. There are two locks on the door. He slides a key into each, and then we're inside. There's a big living room with a large flat-screen TV and two dark-blue couches. On the coffee table is a bag of potato chips and a two-liter bottle of orange soda. There are pink Converse sneakers on the floor.

Girls live here.

I step inside.

He leads me to a small room with two single beds. Real beds—not just a mattress on the floor. One has bright-red sheets with white flowers and a purple blanket that looks brand-new. The other is bare.

"You can sleep there," he says, pointing to the empty one. "Baby sleeps in the other. She ain't home right now, obviously. Tomorrow we'll get you what you need—if you decide to stick around." He disappears for a moment, then returns with a thick blanket. "You can use mine tonight. You hungry?"

I shake my head no.

"A'ight then. Rest up, girl. You must be tired. I'm right outside if you need anything."

I've never slept anywhere but my house. I change into Grandpa's T-shirt and keep my jeans on. I wish I had my pajamas. I pull out red bear blanket and hide it under my pillow.

Then I peek down the hall. Devon's sitting on the couch, the TV glowing all soft and blue. His eyes shine in the dark.

"You straight? You wanna watch TV?" He pats the

cushion next to him. "C'mon."

Things like this don't really happen, do they? To meet someone who takes you in like this even though you ain't family? Who don't mind having you around?

I sit down next to him—but not too close, and he doesn't try. Girls live here. That's good. I picture Grandpa shaking Devon's hand.

Thank you, he'd say. *For taking care of my Punky.*

I lay my head on the cushion. Devon moves down to make room for me. I stretch out and he rests his hand on my foot.

I can hear my own heart go *thump thump thump,* the words *thank you thank you* like a song in my head until I slide into a soft, snug sleep.

9

2700 SURF AVENUE, APARTMENT 6B

Coney Island, New York

The next morning, Devon drives me to a mall.

"You need supplies, girl," he says, and we stride into a clothing store with blaring lights and music pumping like a club. "Let's get you some clothes. It's on me."

"You don't gotta do that," I say.

"Go 'head. You can't be livin' in that T-shirt all the time."

My cheeks get hot. Grandpa's shirt hangs off me, three sizes too big. I look stupid. I pick out two tops, both black, like the ones on the mannequin standing next to me.

Then we head to a department store.

Devon smiles. "So, Michelle from Philly. Wanna get some sheets and a blanket? You might as well stay for a couple more nights, till you figure out what you gonna do."

"Really?" I ask. "You don't mind?"

"Why would I mind?" he says.

Brand-new sheets. Bright yellow with pink dots, and a blanket soft like a kitten. A hundred and seven bucks. Devon doesn't blink.

Then we go food shopping at the bodega by his apartment. It sells everything, even fruit—not like the corner store back home. I get chicken cutlets, eggs, bread crumbs, rice, frozen peas, and a giant bottle of fruit punch. Devon pays for everything, pulling out money from a thick wallet like it will never run out.

"I'll pay you back," I say, but he just smiles and carries the bag of groceries all the way back to the apartment building. "Don't worry 'bout that now," he says, nodding at a guy with bright-red sneakers who stands inside the lobby.

I change into one of my new black shirts, careful to fold Grandpa's tee under my pillow. Then I get to work. I clean up the small kitchen, wash the dishes, and begin to cook.

Dip the chicken in eggs. Then bread crumbs. Put them in the pan with butter. Don't leave them too long or they'll get dry. Save the extra eggs.

I cook up a big pot of rice, then straighten up the living room. Clothes are everywhere—a pair of red jean shorts, a tank top, black boots, a shiny black skirt. They must belong to Kat and Baby—Devon's roommates. I remember what he said about them, about how they don't have family either. I want them to like me. I fold the clothes in a pile on the couch. In the bathroom, I wipe down the sink. There's lots of makeup—glittery lip gloss and dark-black mascara. I put some light blue eye shadow on my lids, just to see how it looks, but quickly wipe it off. I don't want to look stupid, not in front of Devon and his friends.

I bring Devon a plate of food in his room. He's lying on his bed, his eyes glued to his phone, his fingers moving fast across the small keyboard. "Damn, girl, you can cook? Baby gonna be happy."

"I cleaned up too," I say quickly. "I can do the laundry if you want. Just tell me where to take it."

Devon smiles and takes a big bite of rice. "Maybe later. I got some friends comin' over tonight. We havin' a little party for you."

"For real?" I say, my face flushing.

Suddenly the door to the small bedroom opens. A girl emerges. Not a girl. A woman. Or something in between. She's older than me, tall with long braids that fall past her slim shoulders, down across her red tank top. She has sharp edges: elbows, breasts, cheekbones, hips that fill her black sweatpants. Her eyes are messy with black eyeliner, sleepy and puffy, but it doesn't matter. She is beautiful. So pretty that I have to look away.

"There's my girl," Devon says, putting his phone down. "Michelle, this here's Kat."

Kat smiles, but her eyes are hard. "Hey," she says, and climbs into bed with Devon, draping her long body across him. "This is where I sleep. Just so you know."

"Oh," I say, staring at the floor. "Sorry."

Devon laughs, his hand on her thigh. "Easy. She didn't know. 'Chelle, why don't you go make your bed? My boys gonna be here soon. Take a shower and borrow some of Kat's clothes. Make yourself look nice, a'ight?"

I hurry to the small bedroom, suddenly nervous. Is Kat Devon's girlfriend? Who else is coming over? I've never had a party before. Not just for me. I want Kat to like me. I go back to his room. "There's food if you want some," I say to her, then hurry back and open my new sheets and comforter.

A young girl's lying in the other bed, buried under the dark purple blanket. Her face peeks out, chubby and dark—darker than Kat, whose skin is a warm brown.

"You my new roommate?" she asks.

"Yeah."

"Yay!" She sits up, bouncing on her knees, and grins at me—a grin so huge that I can't help but smile back. "We can share the dresser. And the closet too!"

"Thanks." I laugh, relieved that she seems so nice. "I don't have much, though."

"You will," she says, her eyes twinkling, like she knows something wonderful is about to happen. "I'm Baby. I like your blanket."

I smile and spread it out on the bed. It's perfect. Clean and brand-new. I lie down on it, almost afraid to touch it.

"Daddy gonna buy you all kinds of stuff." She smiles. "What's that smell? It smells good. Like a restaurant."

"I made chicken. Who's Daddy?"

Suddenly I hear voices in the living room. The front door closes, and moments later, music pounds the air. Devon sticks his head in the door. "You need to take a shower, 'Chelle. Baby, show her where the towels are. And give her somethin' to wear."

I shower quickly and comb through my hair in the mirror, trying to make it smooth. Baby leaves me a tight pink tank top and shorts with a silver sparkly star on the front. I put them on, but they're too snug so I put Grandpa's shirt over them. There are more voices outside the door. Guys' voices, deep and loud. I peek out and see one of them sitting in a chair, his arm shiny and muscular, his black hair buzzed short and neat. I smile, my stomach flipping, and hurry across the hall into my room.

I don't want to go out there by myself.

And then Kat walks in, holding a big glass of fruit punch. She looks at my baggy T-shirt, sighs, and hands me the glass.

"Here. D made this for you. Drink it," she says.

I take the glass. "Thanks."

"Drink it."

I watch her. "Why?"

She sighs again. Then Devon sticks his head in the door, flashing a smile at me. "Come on out, girl. Everybody waitin' on you."

I take a deep breath and stand up, but Kat blocks the door, pressing her hand into my chest.

"Listen to me. Drink some. It'll chill you out." Her voice is sharp, her eyes cut into me. She's trying to tell me something, but I don't understand.

"What's going on?" I ask, forcing myself to smile, hoping she might smile too, but she doesn't. I stare at the glass, then back at her. The front door closes again. The music gets louder.

"Ain't nothin' bad gonna happen, you'll just have more fun this way."

"What's in it?" I ask.

"Don't tell me you never drank before."

"Yeah, I have," I lie, standing up a little straighter. I push my shoulders back the way Kat does and take a big gulp, bracing myself for the bite of liquor like I tasted from Chuck's stash last winter when he went inside

Boo's to pee and I took a tiny sip.

It's sweet like the punch mix from the corner store back home. I drink it all down and hand her back the empty glass.

"Well, damn," she says. "You didn't need to chug it, but okay. Here we go." I follow Kat into the living room, where a thin sheet of blue smoke floats in the air. There are three guys here. The tallest, wearing a tight white tank top, his shoulders wet with sweat and wide like wings, a shaved head and full lips that look so soft, a cigarette in his left hand, smiles at me. "Hey, now," he says. His eyes shine as they take me in. "Look at you."

My cheeks burn.

This is for real.

I'm in New York. I got new clothes and a place to stay, and now they're throwing a party for me. Devon likes me. So does this guy. He's not a kid, like Tyrell or Mikey or the other boys from school. He's not nervous at all.

"I'm Reek," he says into my ear. Heavy bass slams out of Devon's speakers. The air sweats.

I try to say my name but I laugh instead, and Reek laughs too, handing me a piece of gum. His face wobbles. I try to stand up tall like Kat, but the ground is all shaky and I stumble backward. Reek catches me with a thick hand. The minty gum explodes in my mouth. The music bursts in my ears.

"How you feelin', girl?" he says. I need to sit. I sit on the floor. I shouldn't do that. I look stupid. Reek's blurry in my face. He picks me up and sits me on his lap on the couch.

You see me, Mama? I don't need shit from you. I'm good. I'm better than good. I feel sick-happy, sittin' here on this couch far away from you, with Devon watching me and this guy Reek lookin' at me like I'm really pretty because I am, maybe, and he puts his arm around me and the whole room shimmers. I kiss him. I do. On his soft lips. I never kissed a boy before. Reek's not a boy, he's a guy. Not nasty like Calvin but nice like Devon. Devon likes Kat, I think. Reek likes me.

I smile at him, lay my head back, and the music slows down. I could crawl inside this song, the woman's voice singing just for me: *Ooh, sweet thing, don't you know you're my everything?*

I chew, slow, slower, my face heavy and sinking and I love how sticky my skin feels, I love Kat and Devon where's Baby she's so cute I think I hear Chuck laughing sayin', *You better be good, 'Chelle,* and Grandpa still alive I was happy then so happy all the time I am so happy now I can't believe I never felt so this is Reek right here kissing me like he wants to I want him to think I'm pretty like Kat he's carrying me I want to hug him as he lays me down and pushes when I try to get up pushes me over on my stomach and I sink into myself, into my new bed and blanket and the soft silence that takes me, pulls me down into quiet, enormous sleep.

Am I awake? Something's ripped me open.

Kat is here.

Hold up, yo. Jesus. Drink more. C'mon, girl.

Fruit punch. Cold and wet and pouring down my throat I am so thirsty I feel better okay it hurts okay I want to put my head down okay go back to sleep girl please just sleep okay.

I reach down, touch, and someone's crying.

Reek's lips in my ear.

You did good, girl.

Rest now.

Sleep.

Sleep.

Morning.

Blood on my sheets. Fire between my legs.

I don't have any clothes on.

Baby's awake, playing a game on her iPad. "Hey," she says, but she doesn't look up, just kind of buries her face in the screen like she's embarrassed.

I can't remember anything. The party. Sitting on the couch with Reek. I kissed him. I did. But I didn't do more than that. I've never been with a boy before.

I'm not like that. Am I?

Grandpa's T-shirt is crumpled on the floor. I pull it on under the covers so Baby won't see me naked. I stand up.

Devon on the couch with a huge smile. "Morning, girl. How you feeling?"

Reek behind me. His hand on my bottom. Squeezing.

"Juicy," he says. "Like a peach."

A guy I don't know in the chair, younger than Reek, short, stocky, and loud. "Hell yeah. That's what you should call her, D. Little Peach."

Laughter. Hands slap.

Reek in my ear again. "You loved that shit, didn't you?"

Devon strolls over, gathers my face in his hands like he did at Pink Houses. "You did good, girl. Now you one of us. Last night you did that shit for fun. From here on out, you sell it. That's how we get by. Understand?"

"Little Peach." The guy in the chair laughs again. "Come get a taste."

Fire between my legs. Baby in the doorway, watching me.

I turn and fall to the ground.

10

CONEY ISLAND HOSPITAL

Coney Island, New York

You ask me how I'm feeling, but when I try to speak my mouth won't work, so instead I just look at you through my puffy eyes, hoping you can read my mind like you did the first time we met.

"I remember you," you say. And I smile.

It must be morning, the way the light streams through the window. Everything's white. You lean forward and hold a plastic cup with a straw to my mouth. I take a sip. The cold water seeps into my cracked lips, across my tongue that feels like the size of my head.

"I remember your friend too," you say. "That day in the emergency room. Where is she?"

I shrug and look out the window, the light pouring in like scorching water. I don't want to think about her. I don't want to remember. I don't want to care.

A doctor and a nurse walk in. "Ah, our mystery girl's awake," the doctor says in a thick accent. His face is brown like burned toast, with a thin gray-and-black beard. "That's good. How are you feeling?"

I lick my lips, feeling the jagged edges of my broken teeth. The nurse checks the plastic bag hanging from a tall pole next to me. She stares at me with her tired face and steps away.

"The good news is, your leg's not as bad as it looks," the doctor continues. "You'll have a scar, and we'll need to keep those stitches clean, but otherwise, you should be fine. You're a lucky young lady. The bad news is, we can't do much else for you until you decide to give us more information. We need an adult, understand? There are forms we need them to sign. Otherwise, there's a limit to what we can do. Your teeth, for example. And the pain. I'm sure you're uncomfortable. And we all want to make that better for you. So. Maybe you're ready to talk?"

You clear your throat. "Can we speak outside for a moment?" And you step into the hall with the doctor.

The nurse stomps around the room, fiddling with the IV in my hand, moving your chair into the corner. I want you to come back. I don't like the way the nurse looks at me.

"My leg hurts," I murmur.

"I'm sure it does. Maybe you'll remember that next time."

My face gets hot, and I pull up the blanket to my chin.

"I see girls like you all the time. Comin' in here all hours of the night, all busted up. We put you back together, give you a free meal, free everything, and what do you do? Go right back out there, back on the street. We got real patients to take care of, you know. People who really need help."

She turns to leave, then glances back at me. "You work the corners?"

I don't answer her.

She sighs. "You're no mystery. Not to me at least."

Suddenly the door opens. You walk in, look at the nurse, then at me. She rolls her eyes and brushes past you. "Good luck," she snaps.

Your eyes lock with hers. "What did you say to her?" you demand. But the nurse doesn't answer, letting the heavy door slap behind her as she walks away. *Boom.*

You pull the chair back to my bed and sit down. "Don't worry about her. She's just overworked and tired. Let's worry about you, okay? You're here. You're alive. So let's figure out what we're gonna do. We have a day, max."

I turn away from you, the nurse's words blaring in my head. And then I hear another voice, her breath in my ear, her eyes so hard and pretty.

You better start thinkin' for yourself.

"C'mon, Michelle." You toss your hands up, a hint of frustration in your voice. "You don't have time to fuck around here."

"Keisha," I say. "Her name's Keisha."

"Who?"

"My friend. From the morning we met you. They call her Kat, but her real name's Keisha." I look right at you, a gush of anger and sorrow filling me up till I choke.

"Where is she?"

"I don't know."

"*Who* is she?"

"My sister," I say. "She's my sister."

11

2700 SURF AVENUE, APARTMENT 6B

Coney Island, New York

"Hold still. Damn."

I'm sitting on a hard wood chair in Devon's living room, a bag of fake black hair in my lap. Kat's behind me, pulling so hard on my head that my eyes sting. It's eight o'clock at night. I've been sitting here for three hours, staring at the floor, my body shivering.

"Gimme another one."

I hand her a thin bunch of hair from the bag. She pulls again. I wince. Devon sits on the couch, smoking a cigarette, talking at me. Baby lies next to him in her red pajamas, munching on a huge bag of potato chips. On TV an orange fish is yelling like crazy. "I need to find my son! Nemo! Please!" Baby giggles and chomps another chip.

"You did your thing last night, girl," Devon says. "Good for you."

I shift in the seat. There's a towel underneath me and a dark purple bruise on my right thigh; another on my arm, shaped like fingers.

I had sex with Reek. I must have. But I can't remember it. How can I not remember it?

I thought my first time would be different. That I'd feel, I don't know. Good. Or at least kind of happy. Erica slept with Dez from 23rd Street last summer, and she said it was all right. He really liked her. He'd bring her gummies from the corner store and get all nervous around her. Erica was cool like that. She knew how to act around boys. Not like me.

Maybe it don't count if you can't remember.

I fell asleep, I think. I don't know. The fruit punch that Kat gave me, it made me all happy. Not sloppy drunk like Little John used to get outside Boo's. I was laughing on the couch, all filled up and warm next to him, the music pouring into me and the smoke that looked like clouds floating in the room, beautiful clouds like this apartment has its own sky.

But I don't feel happy now. I don't know what to feel except that something's gone inside me. Like someone stole my insides and I'm empty.

Devon keeps talking. "You'll be with Kat tonight at the Litehouse. She'll show you how it works. Just do what she says and you'll be fine. Remember, it ain't nothin' you didn't do last night."

My head is pounding, slamming in my skull, and I'm sweating hard and shivering, burning cold. My teeth chatter, knocking together like tiny running feet.

I don't know if I should be scared.

I don't know if I should be thankful.

I have nowhere else to go.

On the TV, the orange fish keeps getting lost. Baby laughs and takes big gulps from a bottle of Coke. Her soft belly spills out from the bottom of her shirt.

Kat pulls and pulls, twisting and braiding and yanking my hair. Finally she stops, pulls a chair in front of me, and looks me over.

"You sweatin' like a pig," she says. I shake in my chair and look up at her. "You gonna be sick?"

"Yeah," I say. "I don't know. I don't feel right."

"Hang on a sec," she whispers. Moments later she returns with a glass of fruit punch and a wet washcloth. I drink and she wipes my face, the cold cloth against my hot skin.

"Close your eyes."

I flinch as something brushes my eyelids.

"Open. Look up."

A brush on my eyelashes. I blink.

"Hold your head still. Damn." Kat wipes hard beneath my eyes. "Look up."

"You gonna throw up?" She glances at Devon, then looks at the floor. "C'mon, girl," she whispers. "Almost done."

A brush on my cheeks, sticky goop on my lips. Kat steps back and smiles. "Come see," she says, and takes my hand.

I look into the mirror in the bathroom. Long, thin black braids fall across my shoulders. Light-blue eye shadow. Pink lipstick. Rose-colored blush on my cheeks.

She's a pretty girl. Almost beautiful.

Is that me?

Devon comes in and stands behind me, his hands on my shoulders.

"Look at you," he says, his eyes sparkling with pride. "My Little Peach."

I keep my head down and cross my arms.

"You mad at me?"

I shrug and look away. Am I?

"I don't know why. You should be thanking me."

"For what?" I say, pulling away from him.

"For giving you a way to live, Peach. A way to take care of yourself. You not stupid, so I'm not gonna talk to you like you are. You're a hood rat runaway. You're broke. You're what, fifteen?"

"Fourteen," I snap.

Devon nods like he understands. "I don't know what you runnin' from, but it must've been pretty bad for you to get on that bus with half an address and a pillow. So here you are. And from now on, someone's always gonna try to grab you. The cops wanna lock you up, or they'll just send you back to wherever it is you came from. Or there's always a group home, right? You're too old for a foster family. Not that you want one of those, either. Some old-ass man collectin' that paycheck so he can sneak into your room at night. . . ."

His words burrow into me. I flinch, Calvin's face flashing in my aching head.

"You know what's out there," he continues. "Waitin' for you to come home. Waitin' in the dark."

I turn and look him in the eye. "Shut up."

He looks right back. "No. Because you gotta understand. You *safe* here, girl. As safe as you ever gonna be. Look at Kat. Look at Baby. They're happy, right? Healthy. Fed, clean, they got new clothes and a place to live. It don't get much better. Not out here. Not for girls like you."

"I didn't want to be with that guy last night," I murmur. "I can't even remember. Why can't I remember?"

Devon lifts my chin with his finger. "Look at me," he says. "Best thing to do is forget about it and get on with what we gotta do to survive."

Devon turns me to face the mirror again. "Look at you. Look at how beautiful you are. Can't you see yourself? We gonna make money, Peach. You're gonna make money—you and me and Kat and Baby Girl. We gonna save up, buy a house, get up outta here and onto some-thin' better. We gonna have a good life. That's what you want, right?"

It is. It is what I want. A good life with food and peo-ple who like me. But I can't do what he's asking. Sleep with men for money. It's disgusting.

"I'm not like that," I say. "I ain't never been with a boy before."

"Before last night, you mean." Devon leans in, his mouth on my ear. "You loved it, 'Chelle. You was all like, 'Yeah, baby . . .'"

"Shut up!" I scream, pushing him away. "You're lying! I didn't say that! I didn't want to!"

Devon grabs my wrist and smiles. "But you did, didn't you? You did that shit for hours. Maybe you ain't what you think, Peach. Maybe you mad right now, but you did me proud. I'm proud of you. Hear me? You ain't what you think you are. You're strong. You're tough. I knew it from the moment I saw you at Port Authority. You smart too. Smart enough to run away from whatever mother-fuckers you lived with before. And lucky enough to meet me."

I look at myself in the mirror again, this girl I don't

know. She is beautiful—her hair perfect, her face clean and painted like someone on TV. She's a girl who had sex. And survived. Devon wraps his arms around me. I can hear the orange fish shouting on the TV in the living room. "Nemo! I found you!"

My mother. That house.

Calvin.

Grandpa. Dead.

Maybe I am lucky to be here, with him and Baby and Kat, in our own place, with food in the kitchen and a TV that works. I will make it clean here. Fold the laundry. Make my bed. Fill the air with the smell of something cooked.

"My girls call me Daddy," Devon says. "You should, too, 'cause that's what I am. I can take care of you. I protect you. Understand? Me, my girls, my boys, we all been where you are—and we're surviving. One more thing: I didn't touch you last night. You hear? I wouldn't do that. Not to you."

Devon's eyes flame, like a match in the night. "You want a family? You got it, girl. We right here. And we got a place for you. Just for you."

♫

In my room, my bed is neat, the comforter tucked in, red bear blanket folded in a square on my pillow. Grandpa's shirt is still on the floor in a ball. Baby's getting dressed, yanking a pink cotton dress over her head. There's a kitten on the front. It might be a nightgown. Her hair is in pigtails, twisted and fastened with old-school plastic barrettes like the ones I used to wear when I was young. She looks like a little girl.

"I washed 'em." She grins, pointing to my bed. "Your sheets."

"Thanks," I say, but I don't look.

"You gonna stay, right?"

"What?"

"You gonna stay with us?" Baby fiddles with the edge of her dress. "The last girl, she left. I didn't like her anyway. She wasn't nice. Not like you. She got a different daddy now. We see her on the track sometimes, all busted up and skinny.

"It's scary down there," she whispers. "But we don't work the track. We better than that."

I shiver and pull on the dark-blue jeans that are laid out on the bed. They are brand-new. The shirt is purple and shiny, but not too tight. The satiny fabric drifts across my stomach in soft waves. It's not a kid's shirt, not like the simple black top I got at the store with Devon. I look in the mirror and for a moment I flush with pride. Who is that girl? I turn and try on a smile. Then I see the bruise on my arm.

"Here," Baby says, putting a black jacket over my shoulders. "It'll go away soon. You should stay with us. It's better here."

I search her face. Does she know what I did last night? Did she see it?

Baby smiles again. Her cheeks are chubby, and there's a gap between her yellowish front teeth, with bits of potato chips stuck in between. Her eyes are dark brown and wide open, looking up at me like a puppy. "You look so different. Pretty. When I grow up, I'm gonna be pretty like you."

"You're already pretty," I say. Her face lights up. She bounces over to me and throws her arms around my neck.

"How old are you?" I ask.

"Twelve," she says. She seems younger to me, but I don't want her to feel bad, so I just smile back.

"Promise you'll stay," she whispers, and suddenly

I can feel Grandpa. Like it's his big arms around me, holding me tight to his chest, making me feel like there was nothing that could hurt us, so long as we were tucked in tight together in our warm, dark cave. I hug Baby back, gathering her as close as I can stand. I don't want her to be scared.

"I dunno," I say. "I dunno if I can stay."

She buries her face into me like she's known me her whole life. "It's not so bad here. You got somewhere else to go?"

"No," I say, tightening my grip on her. I have nowhere else to go.

"Then stay. Please?"

My own mama don't want me. But here's this girl. And Devon. They want me. Maybe we could be something. Maybe we can get up outta here, like Devon said. Get a house and giant beds. Get happy.

Maybe I should try.

"For a little while," I say to her. "Okay?"

Baby hugs me tighter, my long braids trickle down my back. I stand up straight and gather her up.

You see me, Mama? I'm not your kid anymore.

At 9:00 p.m. Kat appears in the doorway in a short, white pleated skirt with black and red plaid, flat black leather boots, and a white shirt that falls from one shoulder. Her braids are pulled back into a high ponytail.

She looks rich. Her shoulders are pulled back proudly, her sharp chin pointed out.

She scans us quickly and turns on her heels. "Let's go," she says.

I don't know where we're going. I want to ask. I want someone to explain what's about to happen. I glance at Baby, then at Kat, who looks annoyed. "You good?" she asks.

I swallow and nod.

We descend the stairs with Devon, through the same moist air I remember from the night I came here, when I was half-asleep and hungry, and out into the dark night. Two guys, both in red shirts, open the heavy doors for us. Devon nods at them, Kat flashes a smile. We cross the parking lot, the apartment building behind me like a finger reaching out from the ground. In the distance there's the roller coaster and Ferris wheel with colorful lights turning slowly in the night like a fake moon.

Who's up there, on that ride? Can they see me?

Devon's shiny car. Doors locked. Kat up front, smoking a cigarette. Devon rolls down the window. I grip Baby's hand. She smiles and chews her gum and hands me a piece. I take it in my fist and stare out the window.

The street is very wide. I search the signs. Surf Avenue. 27th Street. A school, a playground, more tall buildings, taller than Pink Houses, taller than anything in Strawberry Mansion. Tall like the buildings in the city. But the streets are the same kind of quiet as North Philly. Deserted except for the corner stores and the boys who stand outside them, mothers rushing their kids home before it's too dark. There's a woman on a corner, shuffling slowly, scratching at her arm. Her body slightly tilted, like she's being pushed by an invisible hand. She looks like Mom.

Chuck must be outside Boo's by now. Does he know I'm gone? Has he noticed?

Kat hands me a bottle of orange juice. "Drink," she says. "You don't look so good."

I take a sip. This time I can taste something else. Like bitter metal. I spit it back into the bottle. My heart punches at my chest bone, like it wants out.

"No, thanks," I say, and give the bottle back.

"You're not gonna pass out, Peach. It'll just calm you down. You look like you about to jump out the window."

"What's in it?" I ask.

"It's just medicine. Like from a doctor. See?" Kat takes a big swig and hands it back to me.

I take a sip. Then another. My heart slows down.

We make a right, past a block of empty houses, past buildings as long as an entire city block, with garbage trucks lined up along the curb.

Then we turn again.

A hotel. We stop at a hotel. The Litehouse.

A small gravel parking lot. Guys leaning up against cars, smoking, watching, nodding to one another. Devon steps out. Complicated handshakes. Throbbing music. Devon barks into the night, a sound like a wolf or bear, and the other men bark back. I shiver, keep my head down, and follow Kat, her skirt swaying as she walks through the lot and up the rusty staircase to the second floor, where there are two other girls perched outside the open doors of hotel rooms. Baby waves, walks down the outside balcony to the last room, and disappears.

Wait. Please. Not yet.

Kat leads me into Room 5. The walls are a sick

yellow, the color of rotting teeth. There are two beds, a limp pillow on each, and an old dusty TV plopped on a chair in the corner. It smells like smoke and salt, like a filthy ocean.

"A'ight!" Kat claps her hands once—loudly—like a coach. "This is how we do. Tricks don't pay us direct. They pay the daddies outside so we don't gotta deal with no money, which is good because tricks always try to get over. Not the regulars, 'cause they know how it work, and they know they'll get their ass beat if they try to scam. But the tricks we don't know? Those the ones you gotta watch."

Kat talks at me, fast and clear and hard. Her hands too. Pointing to the bed, explaining. She fishes in her silver bag. A small knife. She puts it under the mattress. More talking. She pulls out two pills and a bottle of orange juice. She swallows one, breaks the other in half and hands it to me.

"Here. You need to calm the hell down."

She blots my face, shakes the front of my purple shirt. It's wet beneath my armpits, dark like a bruise.

"What is it?"

"It'll help you maintain. Anything goes wrong, we yell

for Daddy. He and his boys'll be up here in a second. Girls out there on the track, they ain't got no daddy lookin' out, not really. Once you in a car with a trick, he can do whatever he wants and nobody gonna help you. Up in here, though, we covered. Shit goes wrong, you just yell."

I don't understand what she's saying.

What do you do if you're in trouble?

I want to go home.

No. Not home. Just somewhere else.

I can't do this. I can't.

Kat steps toward me.

"You straight?" she says.

I shake my head. *No.*

"I gotta go," I say.

"Sit down."

"No. I want . . ." I glance at the door. Outside, someone laughs. A girl.

Where's Baby?

Kat grabs my wrist. "C'mere."

She drags me to the window, shoves back the curtain so I can see the parking lot.

"You see those guys out there? They all Bloods. This

whole damn town is Blood. Every red shirt you see, every red sneaker. They run shit here. You do what you told, they'll kill for you."

Kill for me. Like Grandpa. There are at least ten guys out there, all bigger than Calvin. Bigger than Mama. Bigger than anyone who'd ever try to mess with me again.

"But you try to take off? They'll beat your ass 'cause you'll get us all locked up. Understand? Every single one of them. If you lose your shit and go runnin' out that door lookin' for fuckin' Batman to come up in here and save your ass, you gonna get beat. And then I'm gonna get beat for not beatin' you myself."

"Bloods?" It burns between my legs.

"Yeah. Bloods. You ain't got gangs where you come from? You see red on a guy? Blood. You hear them do that howl? Blood. They're everywhere. And they know who we are. We run with them. We're Blood too."

She pulls mc back to the bed and takes my hands. "Take the pill. Drink your juice. In five minutes, you won't feel so scared."

Kat's eyes burn into me. Small beads of sweat dot her forehead. She grips my shoulders and kneels in front of me. "Please."

"I ain't a junkie," I say, staring at the pill.

"Me neither," she snaps.

I swallow it, gulping down the juice. Kat sighs deeply, rubs her forehead, and glances at the door like she's making sure no one heard us. Like we've just escaped something terrible.

"Good girl," she whispers, and arranges my braids, her eyes full of relief. "Good girl."

Warmth. I begin to float away. Drift all soft and cozy. Like a hug. Kat here with me. I did a good job.

She looks like a cat. The way she walks.

Do I look like a peach?

I laugh and lie back on the bed, pull down the blanket, smush my face into the pillow.

"Will I remember?" I ask.

"Yeah. But you won't mind so much. Sit up. And do what I do."

Outside I can hear voices. Chuck and Little John sitting on their chairs. There's a knock at my door. And I grin.

Grandpa's coming.

12

June 30

She acts like a doctor, but she doesn't look like one. Her hair is short, braided into uneven cornrows. She's old—older than my mom, and fat. Behind her left ear is a red star tattoo. There's another tattoo on her chest, peeking from underneath her white tank top. A saggy bug—maybe a bee—and two faded words I can't make out. Devon leans against the doorway of the bedroom, watching us.

She uses her hands to examine me. My teeth, my

tongue, my arms. I lift my shirt. Take a deep breath. She presses the bruise on my thigh.

"That hurt?" I shake my head no.

"Good. Lie down."

She pushes my knees apart and looks between my legs. Devon types into his phone, a toothpick in his mouth. I fix my eyes on the ceiling, wishing she'd stop or I could just disappear. I don't want him to see me like this. I don't want her looking at my body.

"Anything hurt?"

I shake my head no. She lifts an eyebrow.

"You sure?"

I nod.

From her suitcase she pulls out a small plastic bag. Inside is something that looks like a bracelet, but soft and wet.

"I'm gonna put this inside you. Like a tampon. After three weeks, take it out and you'll get your period. Understand? I'll bring a new one every month. If you feel sick, or if you don't bleed when you should, tell your daddy and he'll call me. Deep breath."

Fingers. Hold still. Where's Baby?

"You know how to put on a condom?"

I shake my head no. Kat tried to show me last night, but I wouldn't look.

"A'ight. Well, you gotta learn. Kat'll teach you. Always use one, so you won't catch nothin'. Understand? Tricks hate 'em, but too damn bad. They wanna freestyle, they can drive themselves down to the track. All done. Sit up. Take this."

I swallow another half a pill and wait for the warmth.

Devon smiles. "All good?"

"All good," she says, and grips his hand, their chests touching as Devon brings her in for a hug.

"Queen Bee," he says with shining eyes.

He's not wearing a shirt. On the left side of his broad chest is a red star. "Kat needs a re-up on Oxy."

"A'ight."

"C'mon," he says to me. "Ink's waitin'."

I lie on the couch, the man's sweaty face just inches from my chest, the buzzing needle tight between his fingers. It digs into my skin, burrowing like an insect. *Buzz, buzz.* Stop. Wipe. *Buzz, buzz.* Stop. Wipe. Dip. *Buzz. Buzz.*

Flecks of blood hit my cheeks.

"Damn, yo. This girl can bleed. She get high last night?"

Devon shrugs.

The man looks annoyed. "Can't hardly see what the fuck I'm doin' here." Wipe, wipe. *Buzz. Buzz.* "Fuck. Don't get 'em high before you call me, D. They be bleedin' all over my shit."

There are four locks on the door. Four bolts, one that needs a key.

Devon flips on the stereo. Music thunders in the room. He opens my book bag, searches it, pulls out my school ID, and slips it in his back pocket.

Baby peeks over the shoulder of the man tattooing me.

"Aww," she says, and her forehead scrunches up.

"Show her yours," Devon says. Baby pulls down her white tank top.

There is a red heart. And underneath, in dark, flowing letters it says, "Devon's Baby."

Devon looks at Kat. She stands up, rolls her eyes, and pulls down her shirt.

There is a black paw print. Devon's Cat.

Mine will be a peach.

Devon's Peach.

Buzz buzz buzz. Stop.

The ink shoots into my skin, but it's like he's draining me. With each sting, I feel less and less. Like the morning after Reek. Like last night at the Litehouse. A little more of me, leaking on the floor, on bedsheets, on this table, till I am empty as a vacant house. My roof is caving in.

There are four locks on the door. Keeping me inside. Keeping out the world.

Devon comes over and gathers my face in his hands, his eyes bubbling with pride. "You a good girl, Peach. You one of us. You get to work, you make your money, and you got a life."

A kiss on my forehead. I fill up a little. I smile.

Devon cranks the music.

Kat holds my gaze for a moment, then fixes her shirt, turns, and begins to dance.

Devon unlocks the front door.

"You must be hungry," he says, pulling twenty dollars from a fat roll of money in his hand. "Go get us some dinner. You and Kat. You like Chinese?"

I stare at the door. It's wide open.

"Go 'head." He types into his phone, nods at Kat.

"Boost'll meet you there."

Down the humid stairs, through the heavy metal door, into the parking lot. Two guys linger out front, one in a red hat, the other in a sleeveless red basketball jersey. Across to 27th Street, make a left onto Mermaid Avenue.

Follow Kat. She takes big steps, her shoulders back like, *Bring it.* Up ahead there's a line of stores. An old woman shuffles past, pushing a cart stuffed with laundry. We pass a guy on the sidewalk. He's tall, with thick arms and clean red sneakers. He nods at Kat, who lowers her head. Then he traces me with his eyes. I put my head down, too, and hurry behind her.

We stop at the Chinese takeout. Two guys linger beneath a dirty yellow sign that says HAPPY DRAGON. The taller one, with black shorts and a red jersey, steps toward us. "Kitty Kat," he says, slapping her hand.

"'Sup, Boost," she says, arching her back a little. I remember him from last night. He was in the parking lot, howling with Devon and the others.

He steps toward me and pulls down the front of my shirt. The tattoo is slathered in Vaseline. Kat shoots me a look that says *let him see,* so I do. I do what she tells me.

I do what Devon says. I let them tattoo me. He looked so proud.

Boost leans closer and squints. "That an apple?"

Kat takes my hand. "It's a peach," she says. "C'mon."

Inside, a blurry man stands behind the thick plastic window that runs the length of the small room. It's splattered with grease and scratch marks, a stained menu taped to the front. The air hisses with steam and heat. The tile floor is stained and gritty. I don't know what to get, so Kat orders me the same as her. Shrimp fried rice. Devon likes lo mein. Baby likes sweet and sour chicken. A pint of each, slide the money through the small square opening.

Outside again, past Boost, down Mermaid Avenue. A siren wails behind us. The same old woman is pushing her laundry, the wheels squeaking creepily, her head bundled in a white scarf.

Through the heavy metal doors, past the boys outside. Up the stairs.

Our footsteps echo. Kat speaks softly. "Remember, they all wear red. Understand? The tattoo, it tells them you belong here."

∽

Night.

Room 5.

I take the pill and drink the juice and wait for the warmth to swallow me. Kat takes hers, too, and we sit together on the edge of the bed. Waiting.

"Where do they come from?" I ask.

"Who?"

"The men."

"The tricks?"

"Yeah. How do they know where to find us?"

Kat stands, checks herself in the long mirror by the door. Dark-blue jeans like tights, ankle-high boots, a white shimmery top draped across one shoulder. She arches her back, like she's practicing. "Online mostly. Daddy sets it up. That's why he always checkin' his phone."

"How much do they pay?"

"Depends. Daddy takes care of the money. Why you askin' so many questions?"

I'm starting to feel warm. "Sorry," I say, and I laugh a little though I'm not sure why. "But we're saving, right? He said we're saving money, so we can go some-where better. All of us."

She shrugs.

"We're gonna save up, right? So we don't gotta do this?"

I picture a big house with grass and food inside.

"Where will we go?"

But Kat doesn't answer. A shadow falls across her face, sits on her shoulders. They sag.

My eyes are dissolving. The room gets soft, my blood all cozy in my veins.

Knock knock.

Kat draws a smile on her face. Her skirt flips all happy-like as she opens the door.

"Hey, sweetie," she purrs, and trails her long fingers down his shirt.

There is a man, a white skinny man with baggy light-blue jeans and a bony face that looks like it might cave in. Behind him in the darkness on the gravel by the road, in this place called Coney Island, with its fake moon, are Devon, Boost, Reek, and the others. One of them barks into the night. The others answer.

You see me, Mama? You see me, Calvin? Here I am, circled by guys who want me to be here. Devon wants me here. He put his name on me.

Try to touch me now. I dare you.

"What's wrong with her? She don't do nothin'."

The trick lies on top of me, pressing me into the saggy mattress.

We are naked. I can feel him down there. I don't look. I don't move. Just hurry up, please, and get off me.

His hands grab at me. His sticky skin clings to me like we're glued together. He kisses, licks my face, wiggles around. The pillows smell like smoke and a thousand sweaty men. His breath is rotten and hot.

Shove. Shove. Shove.

It burns so bad between my legs. It hasn't stopped, not since three days ago when I had sex with Reek. Hold still. Just hold still and he'll finish.

"Oh, c'mon. You gotta be kidding me."

Kat lies next to us, strokes his sweaty back, and glares at me. "She's just new, baby. She learnin'. C'mere. I'll take care of you."

The man peels himself off me and I roll onto my belly, smushing my face into the pillow. My tattoo is raw against the scratchy sheets, still scabby like a wound.

"I ain't payin' for that," he snaps, climbing onto Kat. "I didn't come here to be no teacher." And then he's moving fast on her, her legs up around his back, her mouth saying words—embarrassing words that make me want to hide.

Harder.

You like that?

"Yeah, girl," the tricks yells out. I close my eyes, but Kat's sharp elbow hits me.

Sit up. Pay attention. Her mouth keeps talking to him, but her eyes lock with mine and I can see deep inside them, to the tiny corner where maybe she can curl up like I wish I could, away from him. Away from what he's doing to her.

I watch them, Kat pinned beneath the man's pink bony body, and pull the sheet over my own.

"You can't do that again," Kat commands once he's gone. "You gotta learn to act the part. Word gets back to Daddy that you ain't doin' shit, he gonna come down on both of us. Take another half a pill if you need to. Whatever. Just quit actin' so sad. Tricks, they want happy. They want girls that smile and know what they doin'. Understand? That's how we get paid."

I swallow another half. It fixes me right up so I'm not too scared. Like Kat. I gotta be like Kat.

"He was nasty," I say. I don't want him shoving himself into me.

"Yeah, he is. He don't know what he doin', neither. But it don't matter. You gotta pretend, Peach. You wanna get outta here? Then you gotta work. You ain't gotta like it. You just gotta act like you do. Think I like doin' this?" Kat pulls her shirt on, kicks the side of the bed with her bare foot. "I hate it. But they don't ever know that. Far as they can tell, seein' them is the best damn part of my night. That's how we do, Peach. That's how *you* gotta do if you wanna survive."

Kat's smart. I'll try to do what she tells me.

"Okay," I say.

And when next trick comes, I smile really big. So big that Kat laughs. The trick looks at me like I'm crazy, then at Kat.

"Guess she happy to see you." Kat grins. And he smiles at us too.

He turns me on my stomach. I wince. It burns, but not as bad as it did before. I clench my eyes shut and count in my head.

One. Two. Three. Four.

He keeps going. I try to say the words that Kat would say.

"That's good," I mumble at the pillow.

Five. Six. Seven.

I'm gonna be sick. I look at Kat.

Eight. Nine.

She looks at me.

Ten.

Throw-up fills my mouth. I spit onto the pillow. More of me, leaking out.

Eleven. Twelve.

"Stop, yo. She's sick," Kat says. But he doesn't.

Thirteen. Fourteen. Fifteen.

On and on, the counting drones till I'm slimy with his stink and sweat, my mouth nasty from puke. Even my blood is filthy.

Twenty-seven. Twenty-eight. Twenty-nine.

Kat shakes her head, her lips tight and angry.

Finally, finally, he's done with me. I don't move. I am pounded flat. Once he leaves, Kat covers me with a sheet and hands me a cold, limp washcloth.

"Wipe your face," she tells me, then goes to the door and yells for Devon, but Boost and Reek show up instead.

Reek. He doesn't even look at me.

"That trick ain't right," Kat says, her chin pointed up at Boost, who towers over her.

"What he do?" he asks. "He hit her?"

"Nah. He's just . . . rough."

Boost shrugs. "It's a rough game." Kat rolls her eyes. Then Baby walks in.

I sit up and cover myself with the sheet. "Hey," I say to her, forcing a smile.

She wrinkles her nose. "You don't look so good. It stinks in here."

"I'm okay," I lie. I don't want her to be scared. I try to stand up, but I fall back on the bed. It creaks beneath me like it's sore.

"C'mon." She smiles, and puts her hand on my bare shoulder. "Let's go home."

Then Devon is here, kneeling in front of me. "You good?" he asks, his voice soft like a pillow. I nod.

"Good girl. C'mon. We done for the night anyway."

⁊

We drive home at four a.m. Baby falls asleep in the car, her head leaning heavily on my shoulder. My eyes droop, too, the Ferris wheel turning in the foggy distance. I need to sleep.

Kat showers first. Then it's Baby's turn, but she's already in bed on her stomach, her mouth open, snoring softly, her hand in a fist by her face. I try to wake her, but she won't budge, so I cover her instead.

Devon brushes his teeth, spits in the sink, rinses thoroughly. He kisses my forehead and goes to bed with Kat.

I climb beneath the hot water. It singes the peach on my chest like a wet flame. I plunge into the heat and let it burn me away until I'm clean.

I wake up at four p.m., hungry and fuzzy and cold. Baby's still asleep. There's a towel tacked across our window. Daylight leaks around the edges.

There's not much in the kitchen: a bag of Doritos, leftover Chinese food, a bottle of Coke. Kat's on the couch watching TV. She looks different without makeup. Soft and cozy in Devon's big sweatpants and T-shirt. She doesn't talk to me, so I sit on the other end and eat the rice cold from the container. She flips channels and sighs like she's bored. Or annoyed.

Devon wakes at five p.m. Baby sleeps till six p.m. I eat more rice, sit on the couch, and try not to bother anyone.

A knock on the door. Boost strides in with the short, loud boy who called me Little Peach. Complicated handshakes. A paper bag tossed on the table. Music pumps. They plop down on the couch and lean back like they're home.

Kat emerges from the bathroom, painted and smiling. She sits next to Boost. I go to my room and close the door.

We leave at eight p.m., out into the orange fading sky. Baby munches on M&M's in the backseat, a bottle of Coke between her knees. Devon nods to the music, his phone in one hand. Always.

Room 5. Kat. Take your medicine. Drink your juice.

I swallow.

Wait.

Warm.

Smile.

Knock knock.

❦

Two a.m.

It starts with muffled voices through the thin walls of Room 5. Arguing. A girl's voice rising. Something thumps. Then she starts to yell.

Kat puts a finger to her lips. The trick is in the shower. We creep to the window and peek out.

The girl bursts onto the balcony. Boost and Devon scale the stairs. We can't make out what she's saying, but her face is twisted up. She lunges for the stairs, but they surround her.

"I ain't doin' this!" she cries, reaching out to Devon, who backs away as Boost slams his palm into her cheek. She hits the floor with a wet thud, a pile of hair and bone. Boost grabs her ankles. Her face drags along the floor, a chunk of dirty meat, and disappears behind the door of Room 2.

Behind us, the shower switches off. The trick emerges, steaming and hosed off. Kat and I lock eyes. Then we turn, arch our backs, and smile.

The next morning, Devon comes in and sits on the edge of my bed. He brushes the braids from my face, looks at me with those eyes that say, *Hush now, Little Peach.*

"I'm sorry you had to see that."

I don't know what to say, so I pull my blanket tight against my chin. I can still hear the slap against her face, the way she fell so hard against the ground.

"She would've gotten us all locked up. Understand? They would have taken you away. Taken Baby away. You don't want that, do you?"

Baby's dead asleep; her chunky arm hangs limply off the bed.

No. I don't want anything bad to happen to her. To any of us. But I don't want the other girls to get hurt, either.

I haven't even met the others. Kat knows them all. But to me they're just the shadows I see when I walk up the rusty stairs to Room 5. They don't talk to me yet.

"I had no choice. It's my job to take care of us. That's what daddies do."

Devon rises, takes my hand. "C'mon. You wanna sleep with me tonight?"

I search his face. My head hurts. I'm tired. I can't make sense of this. "He didn't have to hit her like that."

Devon sits on the edge of my bed again. "That girl

wasn't right, Peach. She wasn't like you and Kat. Or Baby. You girls can hold it together. That's why you're here. With me. Girls like her? They're dangerous. I'm here to keep you safe. C'mon. When I was little, my mama used to let me and my brother pile into bed with her when shit got bad. She called it the puppy pile. I think tonight's one of those nights."

Kat's already asleep. I climb next to her and press my head against Devon's chest. He lays his hand on my back, gently, and hums in the fading darkness. It will be dawn soon.

"Kat says you're doing good. Next week, you'll get your own room at the hotel."

He's proud of me. I can tell.

I close my eyes. His heart beats slow and steady. *Thump thump.*

Devon's voice is soft and warm. It curls into my ear. I sink into the mattress, his hand on my back, Kat sleeping behind me.

"Someday, Peach. We'll be outta here. Off to somewhere beautiful," he says. "The most beautiful place you've ever seen."

I am alone in Room 4.

I gulp down my juice and wait for the heat that holds me tight from inside.

The pill is magic. It helps me not be scared.

Kat's in Room 5. Baby's in Room 3. Papery walls between us. I want to tell Baby to tap if she gets scared. But I don't think she does. It's hard to see inside her.

In the afternoon, at home before we leave, we sit on the couch and watch TV. Baby's always happy then, her eyes wide and sparkly. She eats Doritos and sits on Devon's lap and nuzzles her face into his neck. He pats her, checks his phone while she watches *Finding Nemo* until Kat turns it off and tosses the remote on the floor.

"I can't take that shit no more," she snaps. "Can't you watch something else?"

"Why you always turn it off?" Baby whines. "It's the best part! Nemo's daddy's gonna lose it!"

"You too old for that stupid-ass movie," Kat continues, banging around the kitchen. "You know you ain't actually a baby. That's just what we call you."

Baby grins. "You ain't a cat, neither." She jumps up,

sticks her arm through the neck of her shirt so her shoulder's hanging out. She puts a hand on her hip and strides across the room in big, exaggerated steps. Her pudgy nose sticks in the air.

She winks at me. "Guess who I am?"

"Shut up," Kat barks. Devon lets out a big laugh.

Baby tosses her imaginary hair back. "I'm Kat. I'm the shit. Don't you think I'm hot?"

"Shut up," Kat snaps.

"You shut up," Baby replies, and Kat grabs her shirt. Baby squeals and dashes down the hall, Kat right behind her.

"Imma get you, girl!" Kat cries with a small grin.

They laugh like sisters, Baby running back through the kitchen, into Devon's room. They crash together on the bed. Baby squirms and giggles and Kat pins her down.

I want to laugh too. I want to chase after them, but instead I glance at Devon, who winks at me. "C'mere," he says, and I curl into him. "You happy?" he whispers.

I am. When we're all together like this. At home, where it's quiet and cool.

Baby's happy, too, in those short hours before we

leave. But her eyes change once we're in the car, waxy and dull, like she's not really in there.

At night in Room 4, I can hear Kat sometimes, making noises through the papery wall. I wonder if she can hear me too. Pretending. Trying to sound like she does. The men come one by one. Tall, fat, skinny, sweaty, chatty, silent, huge. They act like they know me, pulling me close to their skin. Sometimes they smoke the tiny white pebbles Daddy sells them—like Mama did. Crack, I think. I don't ask. I don't want to know. Their lighters *click click*, the flame plunging down into the glass tube. If I'm lucky, they go to sleep, their milky eyes half-open. I pull the sheets down, take off my shirt, smudge my lipstick, and when they wake up I pretend we were together.

They're too stupid to know that I'm lying.

Was it good? they ask.

The best, I say, and force myself to kiss their rotten mouths that taste like ash. Most of them are junkies, like Mama and her friends. Just like Calvin.

I'll never be a junkie. I will never smoke those rocks or shoot myself up.

But sometimes the men don't sleep. They climb and claw and feed on me, their breath like dirt, their mouths like gaping caves.

The pill is magic. It fixes me, like medicine. I can crawl inside my head where nothing hurts. I can say the right things and sound like Kat docs. I can hold still and float away, float to where it's warm and it's just me and Kat and Baby, and my daddy standing guard.

I like hearing Kat through the wall, because I know she's right there, doing the same thing I am. And if she can do it, so can I.

I listen for Baby too. But she never makes a sound. I hope she's okay. I want her to be safe. I don't want anyone touching her, but she doesn't seem scared, so I don't say anything. I wouldn't know what to do, anyway.

In between tricks, me and Kat meet on the balcony. Sometimes the other girls come out, too, and talk to us. There are three: Candy and Rosie and Sweetie. Candy's very tall, with a perfect pointed nose. Sweetie is shorter, with round hips, her belly button peeking from beneath her pink shirt. Rosie doesn't say much. She stands apart, her head hanging on her long neck. We wave to Devon and the other men, flecks of red in the night, who shout our names.

"Kitty Kat! Li'l Peach! Sweetie Sweet! Rosie Girl!"

But we don't see Baby. She never comes out. Not until we leave to go home.

I wonder if she takes the pills too. But Kat says no.

"She don't need 'em."

"How come?"

Kat shrugs, takes a long drag from her cigarette, stares at the Ferris wheel turning in the distance. "She don't know enough to be scared."

"I wish I was like that," I say. And Kat shoots me a sharp look.

"Don't be stupid," she snaps, flicking her cigarette into the night.

"I'm not," I murmur.

Sweetie laughs and bites into her candy bar. "You harsh, girl."

Kat rolls her eyes, pulls at her white skirt. "Ain't no point being soft. Soft things die. Hard things survive. And I ain't dying. Not from this shit at least."

"Tell 'em, Kat," says Sweetie.

I want to be hard, like Kat and Sweetie. I swallow and stand up straight.

"Gimme a smoke," I say. Kat lights one, hands it to me. I breathe it in, like Kat does. My eyes burn and I hold the smoke in my mouth. But I do not cough.

"That's more like it," says Kat.

"Hell yeah," says Sweet.

"Yeah," I say.

And we stand together in the hot night.

The tricks who see Baby are different.

There's one who comes every Tuesday. He doesn't have a car. He just walks up from the dark, out of nowhere. He's old—like fifty—with droopy white skin and thin hair combed across his shiny head. His body looks like a barrel, shoulders hunched, a fat belly hanging over his loose faded jeans. He brings her presents. Stupid stuff wrapped in little-kid paper with the alphabet or animals on it.

He doesn't look at us other girls. Like he's scared of us. The tricks we see, most of them swagger down the hall and talk to us like they're kings, like they're our boyfriends. But this guy, he hangs his head and hurries by like he can't get far enough away.

Sometimes Kat messes with him. She puts her hand

on his bottom and squeezes.

"We ain't gonna bite," she'll half growl, half flirt.

His pale cheeks get all pink, his eyes dart around, and his fingers twitch in his pockets.

"Leave me alone," he murmurs, and walks faster.

Tonight Kat yells "Boo!" at him, and he actually jumps. The girls fall out laughing, but not me.

"You better be nice to her," I whisper. He stops in his tracks and looks at me for a second, his eyes all wide like he can't believe what I just said.

"Nice to her? I love her."

The hair on my neck stands up and I want to push him, kick him, tell him get the fuck away from her.

On the nights he comes, Baby brings his presents home. Coloring books. Crayons. Tiny stuffed animals. I tell her to throw them out, but she stuffs them under her bed and acts like she won't play with them. Sometimes, when she thinks we're not looking, I see her on her stomach on the floor, coloring Elmo's face, nuzzling a fake little puppy.

There's something wrong with him. When he's with her, I listen close through the wall, ready to help her if she needs me. But her room's silent. Always silent. Like everything's just fine.

Baby, with her faraway eyes. I wonder where she goes inside herself.

On Sunday morning when we get back from the Lite-house, Baby announces she wants pancakes, so we walk to the bodega for supplies: eggs, Bisquick, syrup, butter, and more milk. Kat strolls ahead in her sandals and purple toenails, her hips swing back and forth in Devon's rolled-up red basketball shorts, and a white tank top low enough to show her tattoo.

The sidewalks are empty. It's four thirty a.m.

"It's too hot out here," Baby grumbles. She lags behind us, dragging her feet down 27th Street.

"You walk faster, we'll get there faster," Kat replies. "You the one who wanted pancakes."

Kat's got a little bounce in her step. Me too. It feels good to be outside in the air, with no one else around. Too late even for tricks and junkies, too early for every-one else. Baby looks behind us toward Surf Avenue and the amusement park in the distance. Two seagulls pick at a banana peel in the street.

"Can we get ice cream?" she asks.

"No," Kat says.

"Why not?"

"'Cause . . . I don't know. 'Cause you're annoying."

"I bet the kids who ride on the Wonder Wheel get ice cream."

Kat rolls her eyes. "Not if they're annoying."

Baby nudges me. "Peach wants some, too, right? Who cares anyway? Daddy won't mind."

Kat throws me a look that says, *Don't tell me you're gonna take her side.*

"It *is* kinda hot," I say, raising my eyebrow just a little. "Baby's right. Who cares anyway? Let's get ice cream."

Kat looks us both over. "All right. I'll get you ice cream if you promise no freakin' *Nemo* when we get home. Understand, Baby? I get the remote till we go work."

Baby thinks. "Okay."

Kat points at her. "No *Nemo*."

"No *Nemo*," Baby repeats with a grin, then skips past us to the corner.

"Oh, *now* you movin' all fast!" Kat shouts.

At the bodega we pick out three ice cream cones from the freezer and peel off the wet paper wrapping as we walk back down to 27th Street. The cones are half-melted by the time we get back to our building, where Queen Bee is parked in a dingy black car, waiting for us. Kat walks straight over.

"What's up?" she asks.

Queen Bee glances over at Baby, who's licking her cone, then says in a low voice, "D don't know I'm here, but—I seen your mama, Kat. On the track, down on Flatlands. Thought you'd want to know."

Kat's eyes frost over.

"You wanna take a quick drive? See what we see?"

Kat nods slowly, then throws her cone on the cement, tosses her braids back, and climbs into the car next to Bee.

I wait on the couch for Kat to come home. It's six a.m. when she finally walks in, her shoulders sunk in, her eyes a little red, Devon's shorts hanging off her hips.

"You hungry?" I ask her. She doesn't answer, just fishes out a pill from her bag, washes it down with water, and slumps on the couch next to me.

For a long time, we sit there saying nothing. Kat puts her head in her hands and sighs so deep her whole body looks smaller when she's done. I'm scared to ask, but I do anyway. "How's your mama?"

Kat rubs the palms of her hands into her eye sockets. Her voice shakes, just a tiny bit. "I haven't seen her in a year. I thought she was locked up."

"Is she okay?" I ask quietly.

Silence again. Heavy silence. Kat leans back and stares at the blank TV screen.

"She works the track, see?" she says. Her eyes are turning liquid from the pill, her voice relaxing. "Up on Flatlands. The track's where they put the old girls, or the ones too crazy or strung for daddies to be dealin' with. They leave 'em on the corners. Certain streets, if you know where to look, you show up on a Friday night and there they are, walking the streets like stray dogs. That's my moms."

Kat looks tired. Bone tired. Her shoulders sag. Her eyelids too. "You should sleep," I say. "I'll watch Baby."

Kat shuffles to Devon's door. "She wants to watch *Nemo*, you let her, okay? Fuck it."

Behind her on the bed, Devon's chest rises and falls as he sleeps. Kat climbs beside him and covers herself in a blanket, all the way up to her head, her knees pulled up to her stomach like a little kid with a bellyache. I shiver and wonder where my mom is right now.

Our mothers, who couldn't find us even if they tried.

That afternoon, Baby cries in her sleep. She sweats and turns and mumbles things I don't understand, dots of sweat on her forehead, her feet kicking an invisible monster. I gather her face in my hands.

"Wake up, Baby."

Her eyes bolt open, her fingers tight on my wrists.

"It's okay. It's just me."

"Peach," she exhales.

"It's just me," I say again. *I'm right here.*

I climb into bed with her and she snuggles next to me, her head on my chest, and listens to my heart until her breath gets slow and she falls back to sleep.

For long minutes, I wait. I watch for the monster she fights in the dark of her mind, and swear that I will kill it if it dares to come near us.

In those moments, I know that deep inside, Baby's scared. Not of the men, not of Daddy or Kat or of me, but of something else. Something that came before us, maybe. I do not ask her what it is. But I know what it looks like. I know how it feels.

A mother who smokes up and steals. A man who creeps like shadows in your room.

Knock knock.

I hold her tight and stand guard.

I'm right here. It's just me.

Sleep now.

Sleep.

Sleep.

Night. Room 4.

I know there will be trouble the moment he walks in. His eyes are freezing. I smile, I coo, I arch, I stroke his shoulder. Nothing warms him up.

I climb into bed, smile again, and call him *baby*.

Nothing. Eyes like stones. They drop on me, hard, and don't say a word.

I wait. I don't know what he wants.

"It's okay," I finally say. "We don't have to talk."

Then he's on top of me, so fast I'm not sure what's happening. He pushes me down, mashes my face into the pillow. Hard. Too hard. I can't breathe.

"Shut up."

I kick my feet, try to reach behind me to grab him. He pushes down harder.

I hear a zipper.

No.

Blood slams through my veins, pumping loud in my ears. I see things. Calvin's face on me. Mama in the doorway. Blood on my sheets at Daddy's. I grit my teeth and push back against him till my mouth is free.

Get off me. Get off me!

I scream it out, as loud as I can: "Daddy!"

He picks me up like I'm nothing and slams me up against the wall. His hand comes fast against my cheek, a wet slap that burns. Then he hits me again.

"Shut up."

I scream louder and kick the wall behind me. *Kat. Please!*

I see Calvin again, the doorknob turning. Me, hiding in my closet like a mouse. Nobody's coming. Nobody's coming for me.

The door busts opens. Boost, his giant body like a truck, slamming into the trick. Daddy's right behind him. Then Kat. Daddy looks at my face, his eyes on fire, and slams his boot into the trick's ribs. He picks me up, like I'm something precious, and carries me outside.

"It's all right," he whispers. "Let me see."

I turn my face. He touches it softly, wipes a drop of blood from my lip.

"You're okay, Peach," he says. "It's not that bad. We got you."

Behind us I can hear Boost beating the man. "You don't ever touch her face, you hear me?" *Bam. Bam.* "You don't never lay a hand on our girls, you stupid mother. . . ."

Bam bam.

I do not speak, but deep inside my heart feels like it might bust open. I am so happy.

They'll kill for me. Daddy and Boost. I wish Mama could see this, could see me in his arms. I wish Calvin was here. I wish he'd try to touch me now.

"You all right?" Kat asks. I nod and nuzzle Daddy. He holds me tighter.

"Good kickin', girl." Kat winks. "Good screamin' too. That's how we do."

Bam bam.

Daddy right here.

This is how we do.

We. Together.

August

I will make us a home.

I am always awake before the others. I gather our laundry, straighten up the bathroom, and creep into Devon's room.

"We need food," I whisper. Eyes half-open, he pulls forty dollars from the drawer of money next to the bed, taps into his phone, and hands me the key. "Get some bacon," he murmurs, and rubs my head with his big hand. "Boost'll meet you there."

Down the stairs into the steamy outside. Surf Avenue is busy with people pushing strollers, carrying folded-up chairs, towels over their shoulders, children in bathing suits trailing behind them, squealing in high, happy voices. Beyond the street, over a sandy hill, is the ocean. I make a left toward Mermaid Avenue, my back to the water.

I don't like to see the kids playing. It makes me think about Grandpa. Even Mama, back when I was little and she wasn't so bad.

The bodega sells everything we need. A dozen eggs, bacon, cheese, butter, bread, orange juice. Boost is outside with a kid they call Fuse. He's smaller than Boost, with a thick stubby body and eyes that dart around beneath the visor of his red hat. I don't like him. He talks too loud, like he's always mad.

They nod as I enter, Boost peeling a giant orange. I shop quickly and hurry back home.

I cook a big pan of scrambled eggs and cheese, the bacon extra crispy just for Devon. Kat comes out, rubs her almond eyes. I make four plates, with toast and juice. She brings one to Devon, who's lying in bed, checking his phone.

Baby's still asleep. I pull back the towel on our window and let the light pour in. I shake her gently.

"Breakfast," I whisper.

"I'm tired," she grumbles, her warm fingers in my hand.

"I made cheesy eggs," I whisper. "Your favorite. C'mon."

It take her long minutes to wake up.

She sleeps too much. I think she'd sleep forever if I let her. But I won't, because it's not normal. She needs to be awake. She needs to eat better. She stumbles to the couch, her face puffy and grumpy. We sit together, me and Baby and Kat, and eat in silence.

Kat curls up her legs, balancing the plate on her knees, and turns on the TV. A girl in a bikini, with orangey-tan skin and big hair, talks into the camera about how her boyfriend just broke up with her. Then she's at a bar with a group of people and a boy with no shirt on and shiny bulging muscles. They get drunk, he carries her home.

Kat rolls her eyes and turns the channel.

"Can I watch *Nemo*?" Baby asks, wiping egg from her chin.

"No," Kat grumbles.

Baby sighs, pulls a chair to the window, and stares at the amusement park in the distance. The Ferris wheel turns slowly, a car ticks up to the top of the roller coaster, then plummets. If you listen carefully, sometimes you can hear the shrieks. People yelling, "Whee!" into the salty air.

"Can we go there?" Baby asks.

"No," Kat says again.

"How come?"

"Daddy says it's dangerous. Too many cops around. They'll snatch you up and take you away."

"But we could be careful. We could pretend we're sisters. You could be my mommy!"

Kat rolls her eyes. "We ain't goin' there, Baby. And I ain't your mama."

Baby sighs and rests her chin on the windowsill. "Someday I'm gonna go, and I won't take you with me."

"Go 'head. See what happens."

"I will."

"Fine. I don't care."

"Yes, you do."

"No, I don't."

Devon shuffles out into the living room. I gather our plates and wash them in the kitchen. Baby bounces over to him, links her chubby arms around his neck.

"Can I watch *Nemo*?" she begs.

"Sure," he says, patting her head.

Baby plops on the couch and sticks her tongue out at Kat.

"Whatever," she grumbles. "Sit on the floor, Baby. I gotta fix your hair."

Baby slides to the floor. Kat combs her hair back

with a fat brush, smooths it with her hands, ties it tight at the top of her head in a round puff of fuzz.

"You pullin' too hard!"

"Hold still," Kat commands. On the TV, Nemo's parents fuss over their unhatched eggs and imagine how great their babies will be. But the mother will be dead soon, and only one egg will survive—Nemo, with his broken fin. Baby doesn't like that part. She closes her eyes and hums to herself so she doesn't have to see.

Kat brushes her hair. Baby winces and tries to pull away. "Ow!"

"Sorry," Kat says. Then, a little softer, "I'll be gentle."

Devon checks his phone. I wipe down the counters, stack the clean plates, and make three sandwiches for later.

"I want braids like Peach," Baby says.

"You only twelve. You ain't old enough."

Baby sighs and leans her head on Kat's lean knee. "I don't wanna be the baby no more."

Daddy smiles down at her. "You always be our baby."

And Kat laughs softly, tilting her face and turning a thought in her head. "Maybe not," she says to him. "Maybe not."

The poster is taped to the window of American Suds. A girl with blond hair and neat bangs, in a yellow dress with tiny white polka dots, grins out at us.

MISSING: CRISTINA WAKEMAN
LAST SEEN ON 7/14 AT GREYHOUND BUS
STATION, ATLANTIC CITY
16 YEARS OLD
$1,000 REWARD FOR INFORMATION
CALL (800) 642-TIPS

The air inside the Laundromat is heavy and wet, our dirty clothes tumbling noisily in the machine. Small shorts and tiny shirts and Devon's red tank tops. Baby's face is inches from the poster, like she wants to crawl inside it. Kat and I stare too.

"She's so pretty," Baby says, touching the girl's face.

"Bet she ain't pretty no more," says Kat.

Boost laughs. "True enough."

"You know who got her?" Kat asks him.

"Nah. No one we know. C'mon now. Pickin' up a blond girl? That ain't us."

I don't know what he means.

"Why?" I ask, but Boost doesn't answer.

"Look. Someone's holding her!" Baby says, pointing a chubby finger. An arm is draped around the girl's shoulder. In the background is green grass, the corner of a white house. Boost shakes his giant head, his lips pushed together like he's annoyed.

"Bad business," he says, and sits on a hard chair next to a mother with a little boy in her lap. She glares at him and moves away.

"A thousand bucks! That's crazy money!" Baby's round eyes are glued to the poster. "She must be famous or special or something, for someone to pay that much money just to get her back. Think they'll find her?"

Kat shrugs and folds her long arms. "Who cares?" she says, but she doesn't turn away. Cristina keeps grinning, frozen and happy in her sunny dress.

Baby's eyes fall a little. "Maybe she just got lost. Like Nemo. Maybe that's her daddy's arm. Maybe he the one lookin' for her."

The mother watches us carefully from the end of the long row of chairs, her little boy fiddling with a book. I smile at him, and he holds it out to me.

Curious George.

My heart catches in my throat. "Maybe she's like us," I say. "We're missing, too, right? I mean, sort of."

Kat spits a bitter laugh in my face. "Look at that girl. She ain't nothin' like us. Ain't nobody puttin' up posters for us." She grips the paper, Cristina's face tearing in half, crushed in Kat's dark hand. The little boy twists up his nose and leans into his mother.

"You only missin' if somebody looking for you." Kat's words slice through the air. "Understand? We ain't missin', Peach. We just gone."

Night. Room 5. Kat burns the end of my braids with a cigarette so they won't come undone.

"I want a whole," I say.

The pill clicks on my teeth, washes down my throat in an orangey wave.

Kat takes two.

We don't talk for the rest of the night, but I know we're both thinking about her.

Cristina Wakeman. The girl someone is looking for.

☙

In the morning I crawl into bed, my brain thick and heavy and thumping. And when I hear Baby dreaming, shouting and tossing and fighting off the comforter, I cover my face with my pillow.

Shut up, Baby.

Please. Just shut up.

September

Kat's not herself.

She didn't eat breakfast today, even though I made banana pancakes. I know she loves them, 'cause she usually eats two whole plates full, even though she says I don't make them right. But not today. Today her face fell down when she saw them. Then she disappeared into the bathroom for a long time. When it was time to get dressed, she lingered in her sweatpants, like she didn't want to leave.

Kat's the one who yells at us if we take too long to get ready.

But not today. Today, I could tell, she didn't want to go.

Tonight at the hotel, I take my pill and wait for the warmth, but it doesn't come. I knock on the door of Room 5. Kat's in front of the mirror, taking deep breaths, her hand on her stomach. She's not wearing lipstick, and her eyelids are bare.

She's shivering a little.

"What's wrong?" I ask. "Are you sick?"

Kat shakes her head, takes a big sip of water. "I'm fine. What do you want?"

"The pill's not working."

"What?"

"The pill. It's not working."

She frowns, fishes in her bag, and hands me the entire bottle of pills. "Keep 'em."

Something's wrong with her, but I don't know what. I stand there, waiting for her to tell me, but she doesn't say anything, just stares at herself in the long mirror, but she doesn't fuss with her hair or fix her makeup. She looks different. Like a regular girl who just got home from school.

I swallow another half, then I feel it. "Thanks," I say, and float to the door.

"You gonna need more and more," she says. Then she turns back to the mirror, her hand drifting to her stomach. She stands up straight, her sharp shoulders jutting out proudly.

"Not me, though. I'm done with all that."

That morning when we get home, Kat showers and climbs into Devon's lap. She strokes his face and smiles at him with eyes as soft as pillows, presses closed lips to his mouth, once, twice, again.

"What's up with you, girl?" he asks.

"Nothin'. I'm just happy. That's what you want, right?"

Devon looks at her, searches her face with his eyes. He sees it, too, the something different. "Yeah. Of course."

"Then tell me something good."

"You my girl," he answers.

"That's right," she answers, kissing him again. "Always."

Kat says, "Teach me how to cook chicken cutlets."

I show her. Dip them in eggs, then bread crumbs. Put them in a pan with butter. Don't leave them too long or they get dry. Dump the extra eggs down the drain. We can always buy more.

Her hands tremble. Her lips look dry. She groans a little and touches her forehead.

"What's wrong?" I ask.

"Nothing. Show me again."

"Are you sick? Maybe you need medicine. A pill."

"I'm fine," she snaps. "Just show me again."

And so I do.

Dip them in eggs. Then bread crumbs. Put them in a pan with butter.

Kat and Daddy close the door to their bedroom.

Something's going on.

I wake up Baby, pull the towel back to let the light in. I make us French toast with cinnamon. Baby lies on the couch and rubs her eyes.

Then Kat emerges with a grin I've never seen on her before. She smiles big, her face all bright. She looks older—but somehow younger too.

"I'm pregnant. Me and Daddy, we gonna have a baby."

Butter hisses in the pan. I drop the spatula. "For real?"

A baby.

"Yeah. I took, like, five tests."

"But . . . how?" I ask. "I mean, don't you have that

thing inside you? Queen Bee said we couldn't—"

"Guess it was meant to be," Kat cuts me off.

I go to her. I want to hug her, but I don't know if she'll let me.

A baby. In our apartment. Tiny and clean and soft. We'd be like a real family then. I put my hand on her shoulder and smile.

"You're gonna be a mama."

Kat's face opens like a flower. "Yeah," she laughs. "Yeah. I didn't really think of it like that, but yeah. I am. You gonna help, right?"

I flush with pride. "You know it," I answer. "I'll cook for all of us." Kat puts her arm around my shoulders. Looks right at my face.

"You will, won't you?" she says. "You kinda crazy, Peach. You got something good inside you."

Kat's never hugged me before. She pulls me toward her for a second, holds me there with her shaky hands.

"Queen Bee's on her way. Boost'll take you girls to work tonight. Daddy's gonna stay here with me, to make sure everything all right."

Baby hasn't moved. She shoves her thumb in her mouth and turns on the TV. She looks angry.

"What's wrong with you?" Kat asks. "I thought you'd be happy. You the one who said you didn't want to be the baby no more."

Baby shrugs and turns up the volume. "You're lyin'. You can't have a baby."

"Whatever. You better get used to the idea. You gonna have to help out."

Kat sparkles, her hands on her belly. Baby drags herself up and hugs Kat. "Congratulations. I guess."

Kat rubs her head. "Relax, kid. It ain't comin' for a while. You still the baby, okay? Maybe it'll be a little girl. You can do her hair and dress her up, like you do with those dolls under your bed."

"Shut up," Baby snaps. "I don't play with those."

"You better get dressed. Boost's on his way."

Kat brings me an outfit—her favorite white shirt, the one that drapes off the shoulder, and her plaid skirt. "I don't need it no more. Take it."

She fusses with me, fiddles with my braids. "They startin' to frizz. I'll fix 'em tomorrow."

I'm happy for her, happy to think about a little tiny infant here with us. But part of me is jealous too. And maybe a little scared. Kat won't be next door at the

Litehouse anymore. I don't wanna be there by myself, just me and Baby and the other girls I don't know that well.

When Boost arrives, she walks us to the door. "Be safe," she says, her T-shirt loose and comfy, her sweatpants hanging easy on her hips. "I'll be here when you get home."

The door to Devon's room is shut tight. He's in there alone, talking on the phone. And though I'm not sure why, I don't want to leave her.

"Daddy's happy?" I ask.

"Of course he is."

Baby takes my hand, pulls me out into the hall. Behind Devon's door, music starts to thunder. Hard and loud.

Like a fist.

"Wake up."

Kat's face shines at me, burning through the fog of sleep.

"What time is it?" I ask.

"It's early. C'mon. I got a surprise for you."

She wakes Baby too. We dress quickly, tiptoe in the

silent apartment. Devon's door is closed. She slips the key into the lock, leads us down the stairs into the day-light.

"Where we goin'?" Baby whines. "Where's Daddy?"

"Hush," she says, taking her hand. Baby's still in her pajamas, me in Grandpa's T-shirt and Daddy's giant shorts.

Kat trots down the street in her sneakers, her long hair bouncing. We head toward the ocean, turn left on Surf Avenue. It's ten a.m. I glance around, looking for Boost or the little guy Fuse or anyone else wearing red.

They're not awake yet—only families, dragging kids with beach towels, and the subway station up ahead with people streaming out of it, pouring like water across the street. We mix with the crowd, with men and women and girls and boys and little kids in strollers. The yellow air is warm, the sun peeking up at us. Kat holds on to us, weaves us through the strangers. A woman with a child bumps Kat's shoulder.

"Excuse me," she says.

Kat steps aside, her face wide and welcoming. She smiles at the child. "Have fun," she says, and the woman smiles back.

We dive through the crowd, down Surf Avenue, until Kat halts us in front of the the amusement park.

Baby stops, her face switching on like a lightbulb. "For real?!" she squeals. "But we ain't supposed to be here. Daddy said."

"It's okay. C'mon. We won't stay long."

"But what if Daddy finds out—"

"Don't ruin this, Baby. You the one always complainin' that you wanna go here. Now's your chance."

Baby's eyes shine up at the Ferris wheel. "But the cops. Daddy said—"

"Ain't nobody gonna take you, Baby. Look at all these people. Nobody even gonna notice you, unless you make a scene. So c'mon. We won't stay long. We'll be back before he even knows we're gone."

Baby doesn't move. She looks at me, then back at Kat. "I dunno. It's bigger than I thought. I don't wanna get in trouble."

I wait for Kat to snap, to hiss at her like she usually does, but instead she wraps an arm around Baby's thick shoulder. "It's okay. Nothing's gonna happen. Just have fun, that's all. Like the rest of these people. Just act normal."

There are lots of rides. Small ones for little kids. Teacups that spin, a small red train, a miniature roller coaster. Kat pulls out a wad of wrinkled cash. "Which one you wanna go on first?"

Baby grins. "The teacups!"

We get in line, wait our turn, but the man looks at Baby and frowns.

"This ride's for children. How old are you?"

"None of your business," Kat answers. "We got money. Just let her on."

"Sorry. She's too big. She won't fit."

Kat shoots him a glare like a punch. "We got money."

"She's too big. Sorry."

Baby's face falls a little.

"You're an asshole," Kat snaps. "C'mon, Baby. We'll find a different ride. This one's stupid anyway."

And so, we wander. There are games to play. Kat gives Baby a dollar. She steps up to a counter, throws a ball at a target, and misses. "Keep tryin'," Kat insists with her new voice. Baby tries again, but the ball plops to the ground.

"This is stupid," she grumbles. Then Kat grabs a ball, scrunches her forehead, and whales it hard at the target. A bell squeals and the whole thing lights up.

"We have a winner!" the man announces. Someone behind us cheers. Baby jumps and claps. "You did it!" she shouts. "You did it, Kat!"

"Choose your prize, young lady," says the man. Baby picks a stuffed giraffe and hugs it tight, her big saucer eyes shining and full as she runs to the next game. "I wanna try this one!"

"You better win me something, girl," Kat says with a laugh, rubbing Baby's head, and my heart lifts up, fills me up till I think I might explode. Baby, in her striped pink pajamas. Kat, with her unpainted face. And me.

All together. Like a family.

You see me, Mama?

"Can I get some cotton candy?" I whisper.

"Hell yeah," says Kat, holding out a ten. "Get two."

And I do. I get two, and I don't wipe the sugar off my face.

For the next hour, we dash from one game to the next. Kat can throw a ball at anything. She hardly ever misses. We win another animal—a huge panda bear. Then we race, all of us holding guns, squirting water at metal frogs that swim across a fake ocean. Kat wins again and the man hands us a goldfish in a plastic bag.

"Like Nemo!" Baby shrieks. "Kat! Can we keep him?!"

"We'll see," Kat says. But I know we can't. We can't keep anything, or Daddy will know we were here.

Then we approach it. The Ferris wheel. The fake moon I see at night.

WONDER WHEEL, it says, in giant red letters. Baby stares up at it.

"Wanna go on?" Kat asks.

And Baby can only nod, her mouth hanging open. "I bet you can see the whole world from up there."

"Go 'head. I'll wait here."

"Come with me," Baby whines.

"Nah. I can't. The baby and all. Queen Bee says I gotta be careful."

"I'll stay with you," I say.

"I don't wanna go on by myself," Baby complains.

A woman standing ahead of us in line smiles with her face freckled and brown hair with streaks of blond. "She can come on with us if she'd like to." Her little boy grins with ice-cream-covered teeth.

"Okay," Baby says, and we watch as she climbs into

a blue swinging cage. The door shuts noisily, and then she's in the air.

Kat and I sit on a bench, the ocean right there next to us. I breathe in the air, the sun that keeps rising, the water that licks at the shore. I wonder where my mother is. I wish that she knew that I've made it to New York, that I have a family. A real family. And that soon we'll move away, to someplace beautiful and quiet.

Maybe I'll go back to school.

I'll teach Kat how to cook all sorts of good things. Just like Grandpa taught me.

And once the baby comes, we'll take care of it.

Nothing bad will ever happen again.

"We should get home," Kat says. She's shivering again, like she's been doing for the past couple weeks. "Daddy will be up soon."

"Let her stay a little longer," I say. "It's nice to see her be a kid, you know? Not just sleeping all the time like she does. Or watching *Nemo*."

"True enough." Kat crosses her arms, rubs her shoulders like she's freezing. "That kid came up hard. You know her father lives around the block from us? He used to score his shit right on 25th Street. Baby'd sit on the step of the Laundromat waiting for him to come back. He'd yell at her, call her names. Forget she was there sometimes. When Devon brought Baby home, her father figured out where she was, and he'd hit her up for money. Tell her she owed him. He got those eyes, you know? All lookin' at her the wrong way, like a trick. Not like a father. That's why she sleeps all the time. I think she still trying to forget."

The blue cage swings in the air, reaches the top of the Wonder Wheel, and starts to descend. We wave. Then we see.

Chubby fingers stretched through the metal. Reaching for us.

A little boy crying.

Baby's face pressed against the side. She's crying too.

"I don't like it!" she screams. "Get me off!"

Kat jumps to her feet. "Shit," she says. She pushes past the crowd as the blue cage grazes the ground and starts to ascend again. "Wait! Stop! Stop the ride! She's scared!" Kat lunges for the man at the bottom, his hand on the lever. "Stop it! She need to get off!"

Baby's eyes are frantic. She's screaming at us, the little boy wailing. "Get me off! I don't like it!"

"Step back!" the man commands, pushing Kat away. "She can get off the next time around."

"Motherfucker," she snarls. "Get her off. Now."

"Step back," he repeats.

Then I see the blood. A dark spot between Kat's legs.

"Kat," I say softly.

"Get her off!" she screams.

"Back up!" the man yells.

"Kat. Wait." My hand on her shoulder.

Baby's cage teeters at the top of the wheel, slowly makes its way back down to earth. The man opens the door, Baby bolts right to us, her face wet and twisted. I open my arms, but she pushes me away.

"I don't like it," she cries. "It's too high." Then, to Kat, "Why'd you bring us here? Why'd you make me go on there?"

"I'm sorry! I thought you'd have fun."

"You wanted me to get scared. I know it!"

"Kat," I whisper. "You're bleeding."

A crowd has formed around us. The freckled woman carries her son past us, hurries away like we're crazy.

Kat looks down.

Baby screams.

I take their hands, through the crowd, to the street.

"Baby, go home," I command.

"I want my fish. I want Nemo! Where is he?"

She won't let go of my hand. I push her. "Go home. Right now."

"You can't just leave him like that!"

Kat and I lock eyes. Clench hands.

And run.

13

CONEY ISLAND HOSPITAL

Coney Island, New York

And then you are there. Your brown hair pulled back into a ponytail, your white coat like a doctor, a plastic card clipped to the pocket.

Daniela Cespedes, CSW.

They put us in the back, away from everyone else. Because I was screaming when we got here, because we busted through the emergency room doors and Kat fell to the floor, cursing and crying and bleeding.

She's quiet now, curled in a ball on the bed. Her

hands shake in silence. Her bloody pants are crumpled on the floor.

She sobs.

Her whole body shakes.

I am too scared to touch her.

A doctor comes in and sits down next to Kat.

"I'm sorry," he says.

Because the baby is dead.

"Get the fuck away from me." Her new voice is gone now, replaced by another. Her words flop to the ground, limp and wasted.

He nods, his lips pressed together like he understands, his eyes resting on Kat before he stands to leave. "You can rest here for a while. If you need anything, Daniela will take care of you."

And then he's gone—the heavy door shut behind him.

Kat's tattoo leaks like a stain from the top of her thin hospital gown.

"You've had that for a while, huh?" you say.

"What?"

"The tattoo. It's fading already." You look at me. "You have one too?"

"Don't answer her, Peach," Kat says. "Don't tell her shit."

You smile at her, pull the blanket up around her quaking body.

"How come she's shakin' like that?" I whisper.

"She's in withdrawal," you answer. "That's my guess. Right?"

Kat shrugs, curls herself up tighter.

"You try to quit by yourself when you got pregnant?" Silence.

"Okay. Listen. There are three men outside, waiting for you. One of them says he's your cousin. But judging from the star on his shoulder, my guess is he's your pimp. He's definitely Blood. And you're gonna be in a lot of trouble for coming here. So how 'bout we talk?"

Silence.

"C'mon, kiddo. You've made it this far. Take a chance. Trust me. Maybe I can help."

Kat groans, a deep, hollow sound that sucks the air from the room. Then she starts to shake again. The tears fall down, crash on the bed, and disappear.

"Shut up," she whimpers. "Please. Just shut the hell up."

You sigh gently, then turn your eyes on me.

"How 'bout you? Is he your pimp too?"

"Don't tell her shit, Peach."

The baby is dead. Kat is broken. I open my mouth to speak. I want to talk to you.

I don't know why. I know I shouldn't. I don't know what you'll do to me. But there's something about the way you look at us, like we're not in trouble at all. Like we're nice girls.

And then I hear another voice, reaching out from a faraway place. From somewhere I'd forgotten, or tried to escape.

Punky, it says.

Punky.

Talk to her. Remember? What do you do if you're in trouble?

"He's not a pimp." My voice is small. Tiny. "He takes care of us."

"He sell you for sex?"

I don't answer. A pimp is a guy in a music video, with a tricked-out car and gold chains. That's not Devon.

You keep looking at me. "Is someone selling you?"

I don't answer.

"Okay. Let me put it a different way. Someone *is* selling you—and that person is a pimp. And I know he's a Blood because all those boys waiting for you two are flagging red."

Pimp. If he's a pimp, what does that make me? I feel like I might be sick. "What's withdrawal?" I ask you.

"That's what happens when you stop taking drugs. You feel very, very ill."

"We don't do drugs."

"Okay."

"We take medicine. So we don't feel scared."

"Okay. Do you want to go with them? With the guys out there?"

Through the small window in the door, I can see Daddy. Boost and Fuse, too, the little guy I don't like. Where's Baby? She must be so scared, seeing Kat bleeding. We ran away from her. We left her there, alone.

No. I don't think I want to go with them. But I can't leave Kat. I can't leave Baby. They need me.

I don't have anyone else.

"Can Kat stay here? Till she's better? I could stay with her."

"I wish she could, but the doctors need the bed for other people."

"Like who?"

"People who are hurt worse than she is. Physically, at least. If you tell me those guys are related to you, I have to let you go. I have no choice. But if you girls want help, let's talk. . . ."

Kat pulls herself up, wipes her face. "C'mon, Peach. We out."

"But maybe we should—"

"Maybe you should shut up like I told you to. This woman can't do shit for us." Then she turns her eyes on you. "They're our cousins. They came to get us, a'ight? I said it. So now you can leave."

"Okay," you say. "Well, at least take this."

Your hand reaches out.

A card. A small white card.

Daniela Cespedes, CSW.

I take it tight into my fist.

"You know where I am. If you change your mind, I'm here."

And then you're gone too—lost in the noisy chaos of the world outside our door. Doctors rushing past.

Nurses in a hurry. Families waiting for people they're worried about. People who are hurt worse than Kat. People who get to stay here, with you—the lady with the soft eyes who didn't yell at us at all.

Kat shoves her feet into her sneakers, yanks her T-shirt over her hospital gown. She kicks her bloody pants across the floor.

"Kat," I say. "Maybe we should talk to her. Maybe—"

"My name ain't Kat, it's Keisha." Her eyes are puffy and wet, the color of a bruise. "And nobody's gonna help us. She ain't gonna do shit but send us to a group home. So let's just go. Lemme tell you somethin', Peach. You wanna survive? You want a life? Then you better start thinkin' for yourself. Don't be listenin' to no lady in a hospital. She ain't magic. Nobody is."

In the waiting room, the boys surround us.

"What the fuck," Devon growls, gripping Kat's arm so hard her skin squeezes through his fingers. "You better tell me right now you didn't say a goddamn word to these people."

Kat looks right at him. "You scared, D? Maybe I did. Maybe I told them everything."

Then Devon's eyes light up. Like a fire. He grips

my arm, too, Boost right beside him, Fuse making fists with his hands, and they lead us out into the hot August streets.

Home.

Kat paces like a creature, her face wet and shaky. She looks crazy. Boost and Fuse stand by the door with their giant stiff bodies and watch Devon, who watches Kat. His face is hard and still. His eyes flame like gasoline, his hands balled up.

The air crackles.

"You fucking crazy bitch," he says to her. "You tryin' to get us all locked up? Goin' to a hospital? What the fuck you say to them, huh?"

I clench my eyes shut, and then I see her: the girl from the hotel, the one who was screaming, the one that Boost put down on the balcony. The girl we never saw again, and Devon's words to me that night.

She would've gotten us all locked up.

"You did this to me," Kat hisses, her eyes wobbling in her head. Her face is drenched, sweat dripping down to her shoulders. "You told Queen Bee to kill it. I know you did. She gave me a pill. She said it was a vitamin."

"What you say to them, Kat?" Devon's voice rises, rumbling like a storm. I cover my ears. I don't want to hear this.

Kat gets up in his face, her head twisting on her long neck. "Maybe I told them the truth. That you killed my baby. Maybe I told 'em I been doin' this shit for five years, makin' you money, believin' all the shit you talk. You been talkin' shit at me since you picked my ass up at that group home. We gonna make money, Kat. We gonna get up outta here, Kat. We gonna have a baby. We gonna get a house. You talk and talk but we ain't got shit. You gonna work me till I'm dead. Till I end up like those girls on the track, all strung out and used up and starvin'."

The words shoot from her mouth like bullets. But they bounce right off him.

"I ain't doin' this no more. I'm done. You hear me? You had no right. You had no fuckin' right! You promised me, D! You promised! You said!"

Boost takes a step toward Kat, then backs away when Devon raises his hand. I wait for the slap, for Kat to crumple on the floor, but Devon pulls her in. She struggles, squirms, then pushes her head into his chest. I don't know what she's doing.

"I didn't kill nothin', Kat. You talkin' crazy. You need to calm the hell down."

Kat pulls away from him, falls on the couch in a pile. "That was my baby. It was mine. I woulda raised it. I woulda loved it."

Devon shakes his head, a thin laugh slipping from his lips. "Look at you. What the hell you gonna do with a baby, Kat?"

"I woulda loved it," she says. "You got no idea what I am."

"Get dressed, Peach," Devon barks. "Get Baby dressed too. We'll talk about your little trip this morning later. Kat'll stay with me tonight."

I don't want to go. I don't want to leave her. But Boost grips my arm, pushes me into the bedroom where Baby's buried underneath her blanket.

"You heard him. Get dressed. Now."

And so I do.

So does Baby. Her hair in pigtails and barrettes. Dressed in her costume: a stupid pink dress with ruffles.

And we leave Kat behind.

She is still crying, crumpled on the couch in her

hospital gown, her hands on her empty stomach, when we step into the hall. She does not look at us.

Boost and Fuse drive us to the Litehouse.

Up the metal stairs.

Me in Room 4.

Baby in Room 3.

Kat's room is empty.

Baby's face is hard—as hard as Devon's.

"I told you we shouldn't have gone," she says, with eyes that I don't recognize, and shuts the door behind her.

Two a.m.

The trick takes long pulls from his glass pipe, the small white pebble melting in the heat. Watery smoke spills from his nose. His eyes sag, and soon he starts to snore.

I take his phonc and lock the bathroom door.

I can only think of one person to call.

Information.

"What city and state, please?"

Philadelphia. Pennsylvania.

"What listing?"

Boo's Lounge.

"Please hold a moment."

Ring ring.

Music and voices.

"This Boo's!" says a man.

My heart throbs in my throat.

"Is Chuck there?"

"Chuck?"

"Yeah. Chuck. Out front."

"Hold on a sec."

Music and voices and noise. I wait and wait and wait until I hear him.

"Hello? Who this?"

"It's me," I whisper. "It's Michelle."

"I can't hear shit. Hold up. Yo, Boo! Turn the damn music down!"

Please. Please hear me.

"Hello?"

"Chuck! It's Michelle!"

"Michelle? Is that you?" His words slide into each other, slow and messy. He's drunk.

"Yeah, it's me."

"I . . . I don't . . . Where are you?"

"I'm in New York. Can you come get me?"

"What?"

"I'm in New York."

"New York?! Your mama said . . . I don't understand. Michelle? Is it really you?" He's shouting now.

"Yeah. It's me. Please. Listen. I think—" I swallow hard. "I think I'm in trouble."

"What kind of trouble?"

I don't know. "I just need help. Can you come get me?"

"Oh, 'Chelle."

He's crying now. Something shatters in the background. "Goddamn it!" he hollers. "Michelle? You still there?"

"Yeah." My head falls in my hands. I sit on the toilet, the phone pressed to my ear, and pretend I'm sitting outside of Boo's with him, like I did when I was little, waiting for Grandpa to get home.

"Your mama, she gone, 'Chelle. I think she got locked up. I asked her where you went, but she kept givin' me stories like you was with a friend or you went to stay with family, but I know you ain't got no family. The house all empty now, 'Chelle. The lights ain't on. I been thinkin' about you so much. I miss you. Your grandpa, he asked me to look out for you, and I tried to, I swear, but . . ."

Chuck keeps talking, the words crashing into one another, breaking up when he starts to cry again.

He can't help me. He can't even talk right.

"I met a lady," I say. "She said she can help me out. But I don't know, Chuck. I need . . . I need somebody to tell me what to do. Can you tell me?" My voice breaks, and I wait for him to say something. *I'm on my way.* Or, *Stay right there. I will find you.*

For a moment, he's quiet, the sounds of Boo's in the background. Music. Voices. Someone laughing.

"Oh, God," he says in a low, weak voice I can barely hear. "I'm sorry, 'Chelle. I'm sorry I ain't like your grandpa want me to be."

I sit on the toilet. He's crying.

"You gotta talk to somebody. Somebody gotta know what to do."

"The lady, she's like a doctor, I think," I say.

"That's good. That's good. She gonna take care of you?"

I clear my throat and fight to steady my voice.

"Yeah," I lie. "Yeah."

Chuck sighs, like a weight's been lifted off him, then he starts to talk again, about Mama and Grandpa and how much he misses me.

"I love you," I whisper over the words that spill from his mouth onto the dirty floor of Boo's, a million miles away from this place, this filthy bathroom, the filthy man on the other side of the door, snoring like a truck, leaking smoke. Waiting for me. "I gotta go. Say hi to Little John for me."

"Oh, 'Chelle," he weeps. "Oh, 'Chelle."

I know.

I wish you were Grandpa too.

I wish he was here.

Click.

On the bed, the trick's eyes open slowly, roll around in his head before landing on me.

I arch my back, toss my braids aside. They are unraveling.

Tomorrow Kat will fix them. She'll sit me on the floor and yell at me for not taking care of them right. Then she'll work each one till I'm perfect.

That's what she'll do.

"Hey, girl," the trick murmurs, wiping his nose and looking around like he's not sure where he is. "We done?"

"Yeah." I smile, in the voice Kat taught me. "We done, baby. It was great."

I walk out and down to Baby's room and open the door without even knocking.

The man is sitting on the edge of the bed. His pants are off. Baby's on his lap, staring at the wall with empty eyes, his arms wrapped around her, his hips wiggling beneath her.

"You're my little girl," he coos. "Aren't you?"

"Get off her," I snarl. Baby looks over at me, but it's like she doesn't see me at all.

"Get out," she says weakly. "Just leave me alone."

14

2700 SURF AVENUE, APARTMENT 6B
CONEY ISLAND, NEW YORK

Seven a.m.

A boy I don't know takes us home in Devon's car, his red hat turned backward.

Baby doesn't look at me. She bites at her finger and stares out the window. When I reach out for her shoulder, she shrugs me off and shoves her thumb in her mouth.

Home.

Up the stairs to the apartment.

Something's wrong.

Music slams the air, the bass punching. *Boom. Boom.* A man's voice growling rhymes over the thick beat:

> *I ain't a killa but don't push me.*
>
> *Revenge is like the sweetest joy next to getting . . .*

Devon has no shirt on, his skin shimmering darkly. The red star on his chest is scratched, a trickle of blood mixed with sweat. He jumps to the music with Boost and Fuse, who yank at the front of their shirts. The air is thick with smoke, a bag of weed on the table.

Devon tilts his head back and barks—that sound they make like wolves. Boost barks back at him, the music pounding, shaking the room, shaking me, like a terrible storm that's about to crush us.

I take Baby's hand. She tries to pull away, but I won't let her go. She stares at the men, her mouth slightly open. They look huge. Skin and muscle and rage.

Where's Kat?

"Go to your room," I whisper to her. "Now."

I creep to the door of the other bedroom. The mattress is flipped against the window, sheets torn off, a broken glass on the floor. The table is cracked in half.

There's blood on it.

My heart pumps hot in my chest.

Devon's behind me. His hot mouth in my ear. His hand on my bottom. I jump. He's never touched me like that. He smells like weed and beer.

"Clean this shit up, Peach. You sleep in here now. Understand?"

His hand burns into me, squeezes hard. I stare at the blood on the table. "Where's Kat?" I ask.

"Clean this shit up." His breath like fire, licking at my face. "I gave you a long-ass leash. I gave all you bitches a long-ass leash, and what you do with it? From now on, we on lockdown. You don't go nowhere by yourself. Clean this shit up and get in bed."

His hand slides under my shirt, squeezes again. I push his hand away. I don't want him touching me like that. Not him. Not Daddy.

"You fucking girls."

Devon peels off his sweaty shorts, tosses his phone on the floor, and walks to the bathroom.

The music stops, replaced by the thunder of a video game. Boost and Fuse sit on the couch. A haze of weed smoke hangs in the hot air that smells like men. They grip the controllers in their hands, gunning down soldiers, blood exploding on the screen.

Their eyes are like guns.

My hands tremble. I want a pill. I don't want to feel this scared.

Something's happened. They did something bad.

I rush to Baby's room, kneel down at her head that's buried in her blanket.

"Baby, listen to me. Kat's gone. I think they hurt her. I think we need to get outta here. Now."

Baby's turned away from me, her eyes closed tight, her thumb in her mouth.

I shake her. "Baby. Wake up. C'mon."

"Leave me alone," she murmurs.

I find my sneakers, your card tucked deep inside where I've hidden it.

"Listen to me. I know you're mad, but you gotta listen. I got a plan, okay? I won't leave you, I promise. But you gotta listen. We can't stay here."

Baby doesn't answer. She sucks harder, puts a chubby hand across her eyes. The sound of gunshots blazes through the apartment. My heart is running, tearing so fast I cannot breathe.

"Baby, please."

Please.

"You left it. You left it there to die," Baby mumbles through her wet thumb.

"What? Baby, you gotta listen to me."

"Nemo. The goldfish. You just left it there, on the bench. It's probably dead."

"What are you talking about?"

"At the park. You and Kat. You just took off and left it there. You said I could keep it. You said we'd bring it home, like Nemo. But we didn't. You left it. And now it's dead."

A single tear leaks from her closed eye. She sniffs, pulls her legs up. "How could you do that?"

She's not even listening to me.

"I'm sorry, okay? I'll get you a new one, I swear. Once we get outta here."

"I don't want a new one. I want that one." She sounds like a little kid, stomping her feet.

"Baby, listen to me! Don't you get it? We—"

"I don't wanna be your friend no more. Just leave me alone."

I sink to the floor, my knees digging into the dirty carpet. I love her. I don't want her to get hurt. But I am a kid too. I can't make her do anything. I can't make her wake up. I clench your card tight in my hand.

"I'm sorry," I whisper. "Baby. I'm so sorry."

"What the fuck you saying to her?" Devon's voice booms at the doorway. I can still feel his hand under my shirt. What's happening? Why is he doing this? My armpits are soaked, pain stabbing at my forehead.

"I was just tucking her in," I say, and try to smile like Kat would, because maybe it will calm him down.

"Get the fuck in bed, Peach. I ain't playin' with you no more."

And he waits until I leave, until I leave her alone in her bed, in the room we used to share, buried underneath her blanket, her eyes shut tight against it all. Devon grabs my arm as I pass by. I steady myself, draw my lips into a smile, and lace my arms around his neck.

I say the words Kat taught me. Stand up straight. Arch your back. Pretend.

"Go take a shower. It's all good," I whisper. And I glide across the floor, past the TV with the men in bloody heaps, into his bedroom.

I shut the door and grab Devon's phone as soon as the shower turns on.

I shiver, a deep coldness creaking through my bones despite the heat, your card clenched in my hand, your words crying out in my head.

The doctors need the bed for other people. People who are hurt worse than she is.

I don't know how to work Devon's phone. It has a large screen with lots of buttons, like a keyboard. I push one, then another, till the screen lights up. Then I punch in the numbers: 911. And I wait.

Outside the door, the gunshots blaze. The shower shuts off.

"911. What's your emergency?"

"I need an ambulance," I say. "A girl's getting beat up."

"What's the address?"

"2700 Surf Avenue, Apartment 6B. Coney Island."

"Okay. Can you see her? Is she conscious?"

"Please. Come quick. She needs help!"

The doorknob turns. I drop the phone and turn to face my daddy.

Devon. The guy who rescued me, who found me in the bus station, gave me food, and drove me to Pink Houses. And when I broke and cried, he took my face in his hands and promised me, *I'm gonna take care of you, 'Chelle. I swear.*

"Thought I told you to clean this shit up, Peach."

I search his face, looking for the remnants, looking for the guy I once believed. He was there yesterday. Everything was okay. But all I can see is the scratch on his chest, feel his fingers on my bottom. The blood on the table. The empty place where Kat once slept.

"Where is she?" I say. "Where's Kat?"

"She's gone."

"Where?"

Devon laughs, but he doesn't answer me.

"Tell me the truth. Tell me what you did to her."

In the distance I can hear the sirens screaming. I don't have much time left.

Devon doesn't answer.

"I'm not going back to that hotel. Baby either. I looked in her room tonight. I know what you make her do."

"What you just say to me?"

"You're a pimp."

His eyes flare in his skull. "I saved you. I don't MAKE you do shit."

"Where is she? Where's Kat?"

"Maybe she's dead."

Blood roars through my ears. The sirens get louder. They are coming.

"I'll tell. I'll tell the cops. I'll get us all locked up. I swear, I will."

And then he's on me. I crash to the floor. Boost bursts through the door, grabs my hair, and pulls me to the living room. I close my eyes, softly, gently, and surrender to their hands, holding on to nothing but the sirens that are coming and the card deep in my fist. I will not let it go, no matter what they do.

My hair is twisting, twisting, a hand on the back of my head, pulling me up, and then the smash of my face into the table. Something crunches, warm and wet down my throat, sharp and hard on my tongue. The shattering of glass. Plunging deep. Burning in my leg.

My face caves in, over and over again into the table, the place where me and Kat and Baby eat our breakfast. But I can see them through the blood, Boost all calm in his red shorts, Fuse bouncing like a mad man in his red sneakers.

I see them now. I can see them all. My daddy too. I

know what he is. And I think the words every time they slam my head.

Thank you.

Because the make-believe is over.

Thank you.

Because at least I know that you don't love me, either.

Thank you.

Because now, I can run.

"Yo, D, you hear that?" Boost says. Devon looks out the window, then at me. Sirens. A broken smile on my lips.

"You little bitch."

Boost picks me up, opens the door, and with a single sweaty heave I tumble down the stairs into the light.

15

CONEY ISLAND HOSPITAL

Coney Island, New York

You ask me to tell you the truth, and so I'll try. I'll try to tell you everything. I'll try very hard to not be scared. I don't have the pills anymore. I shiver like Kat. All the time.

"What's your name?" you asked the morning I came in, your voice all soft and warm.

That is not an easy question. I've been called so many things.

Michelle.

Little Peach.

Bitch.

But my favorite name, nobody will remember. Nobody's left to know what I was called a long time ago when I was little, when I would hide beneath my red bear blanket, the TV glowing all soft and bluish in my toasty-warm living room.

Punky.

Time for bed, Punks. Wanna read a book?

I would give anything.

I think Kat is dead. I think they killed her. She was gonna have a baby. I think she thought that was her way out, her way to save herself, to maybe save all of us. But the baby's dead too. It died right there at the amusement park on the day we got to play.

I don't know if Daddy told Queen Bee to kill it, but it doesn't really matter. Kat thought so. It made her go crazy.

I didn't want to leave Baby. I tried. I swear I did. But I couldn't make her look at me. Her eyes got far away and I couldn't reach her.

She hates me now.

Maybe she should.

⌒

I know that you will take me to a group home. I got no family. There's no one left to love me. That's where girls like me end up: a brick building with other kids that nobody wants. We stay there till we're big and then they let us go too.

I'm not stupid, Kat. I know there ain't no magic place for kids like us.

Isn't.

I know there isn't.

But nothing can be worse than where we were. Nothing can be worse than that, right?

Daddy will know where to find me. He'll know where I'll end up. Maybe someday he'll come for me or he'll send one of his boys. His name's carved in my chest. I can never take it off, no matter how hard I scrub. In a way, I'll always be his.

But for now I'm safe, here at the hospital with you. I will stay as long as I can and I will try to explain.

I think you'll understand, even if you can't do much. That counts for something, I guess—the way you look at me, like I'm not bad. Like deep inside, I'm just a kid who didn't mean to.

I didn't mean to. I swear.

I thought he was my friend.

I'm alone in the room now, the tube stuck in my hand, my leg all wrapped and clean. I can see better now. My eyes are not so swollen. But I still shake. Everywhere. Even my bones tremble.

I want a pill so bad. I want to feel warm again, to float away and be happy.

I'll wait for you, here in the bed. I know you'll come back. And I will tell you. I'll tell you as much as I can.

I will tell you where to find them—Daddy and Baby and the rest. They'll be gone, though. The apartment will be empty. He's smart, my daddy. He knows how to hide us. He knows nobody's gonna look too hard anyway.

But somewhere out there, in this place called New York, there is a girl. I don't know her real name, but if you look closely, if you can coax her over, if you bring her a present and wrap it up all nice, maybe she'll talk to you. And maybe you'll see the red heart on her chest.

"Baby," it says. "Devon's Baby."

She's only twelve years old. She doesn't act scared.

But sometimes, scared is right. I'm scared—now, without the pills. My hands keep shaking, and I can't turn off my brain. It buzzes in my head, noisy and electric.

I don't know if I can stand it. It won't last forever. That's what you say. But it hurts. It hurts so bad like I don't even know.

My name's Michelle Boyton. I grew up in Philadelphia, in a house on North 26th Street. My grandpa raised me. We had food and a TV and blue lights for Christmas.

Maybe someday I'll go back. I'll find my house and clean it. I'll open the windows and let in the light. Chuck will be waiting. I'll clean him up, too, once I'm old enough.

But for now, I'll do what you tell me. For now I am here. It's not enough. But it's something.

The door opens.

There you are.

You sit by my side and take my hand.

"You're awake," you say, and I smile.

✑

I am.

I am awake.

In the United States, the average age of entry into prostitution is thirteen years old. In the New York City area
alone, an estimated two thousand young girls are being
sold for sex. Like Peach, Baby, and Kat, the vast major-
ity are runaways, often from our poorest communities,
who are fleeing sexual abuse at home. Desperate for
food, shelter and—above all—a sense of safety and love,
these girls make easy prey for those who seek to profit
from the sale of their bodies. Unlike a bag of heroin,
a girl can be sold again and again—a steady stream of
revenue for those who "recruit" them.

While researching this novel, I witnessed the selling of girls in the hotels of Coney Island and East New
York, Brooklyn. I spent many hours driving the streets
with an NYPD detective, who showed me the intrica-
cies of gang culture and the sex trade. I also spent time

with two women who had been targeted in the same way Peach was. Both had been tattooed by their pimps before the age of fourteen. Both had been given highly addictive narcotics, making them all the more dependent on their captors. And, like the girls in this novel, both believed that this was the best they could hope for. Though *Little Peach* is fiction, it is closely based on the stories these women shared with me.

How can this be happening in a country as wealthy as ours? The answer is complicated, and there is no easy fix. Child protective services are terribly underfunded. Inner-city public schools are overburdened and understaffed—in some cases, without enough money to even have a school nurse or guidance counselor available to help students like Peach. Finally, there is our criminal justice system. The United States now incarcerates more individuals than any other country on the planet, and most of those individuals are poor, nonviolent, and minority. All too often, girls like Peach are treated as criminals rather than victims, and end up in jail for prostitution or drug use once they turn eighteen.

We can, and must, do better. I do not have an easy

solution, but I put my hope in you, dear reader, that you will raise your fists, rattle the cage, and insist that this comes to an end.

For more information on domestic trafficking and what you can do to help, visit the Girls Educational and Mentoring Services website at www.gems-girls.org.

ACKNOWLEDGMENTS

This book would not have been possible without the help of Sergeant Joe Catapano of the NYPD. I am forever thankful for your time, your assistance, and for your kindness to the women we met.

Special thanks are also owed to the mighty Ms. Patty McCormick, Marcia Wernick, Alessandra Balzer, Chris Calhoun, Dr. Jackie Devine, Dr. Beth Kastner, Bob Reeves, the Stony Brook Southampton MFA program, Annette Triquere, Andrea Davis Pinkney, Kathleen Lynch, Katharine Richards, Heatherose Peluso, Bill Holland, Irene Schulman, and Nick Spathis.

I am incredibly grateful to my family—Erin and Chris, Mom, Jill and Abigail—who stand by my side every single day.

Above all, to Miracle and Jen, for trusting me with your stories. I hope I've done them justice.